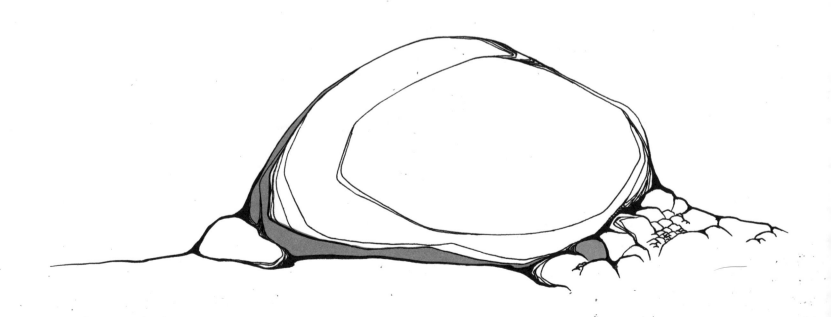

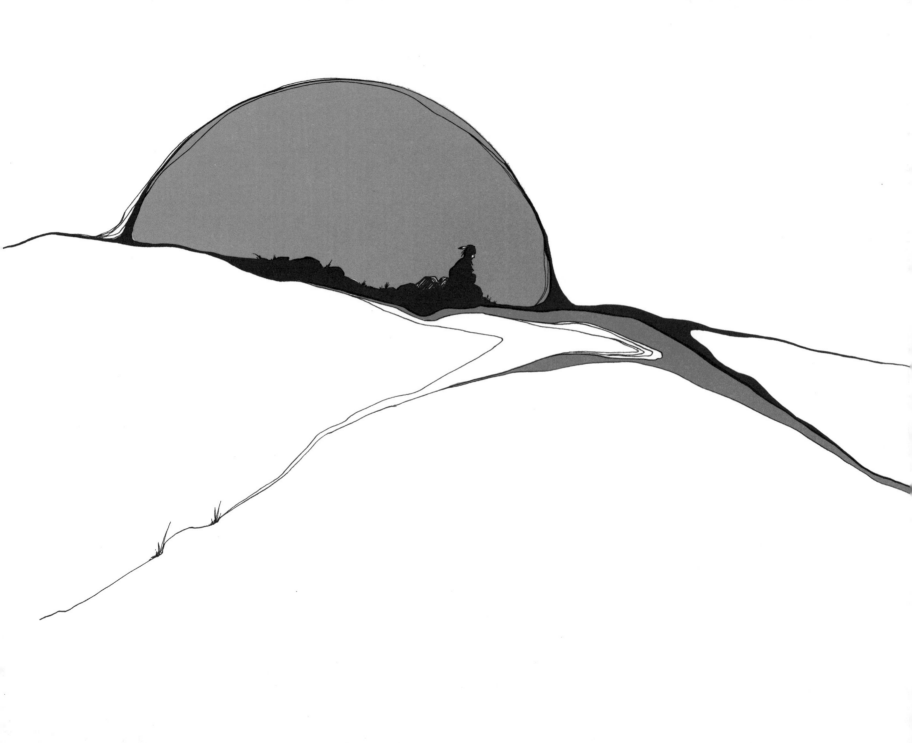

EVERYBODY NEEDS A ROCK

by Byrd Baylor with pictures by Peter Parnall

Aladdin Paperbacks

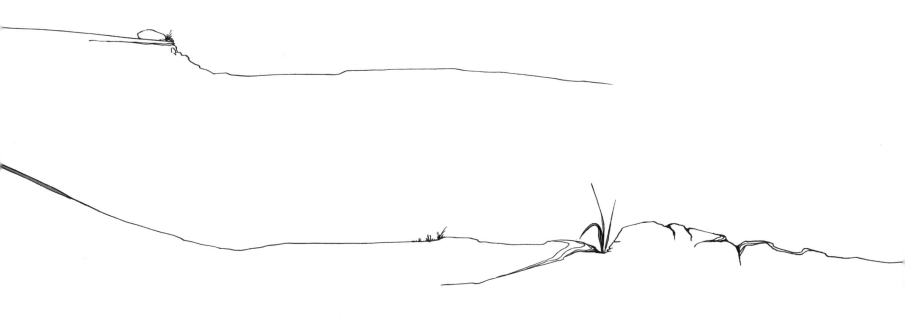

Aladdin Paperbacks
An imprint of Simon & Schuster
Children's Publishing Division
1230 Avenue of the Americas
New York, NY 10020

First Aladdin Paperbacks edition, 1985

Also available in a hardcover edition from
Atheneum Books for Young Readers

Manufactured in the United States of America

17   19   20   18   16

Library of Congress Cataloging-in-Publication Data

Baylor, Byrd.
Everybody needs a rock.

Reprint. Originally published: New York : Atheneum,
c1974.

Summary: Describes the qualities to consider in
selecting the perfect rock for play and pleasure.
[1. Rocks—Fiction]   I. Parnall, Peter, ill.
II. Title.
[PZ7.B3435Ev   1985]   [E]   86-22252
ISBN 0-689-71051-8

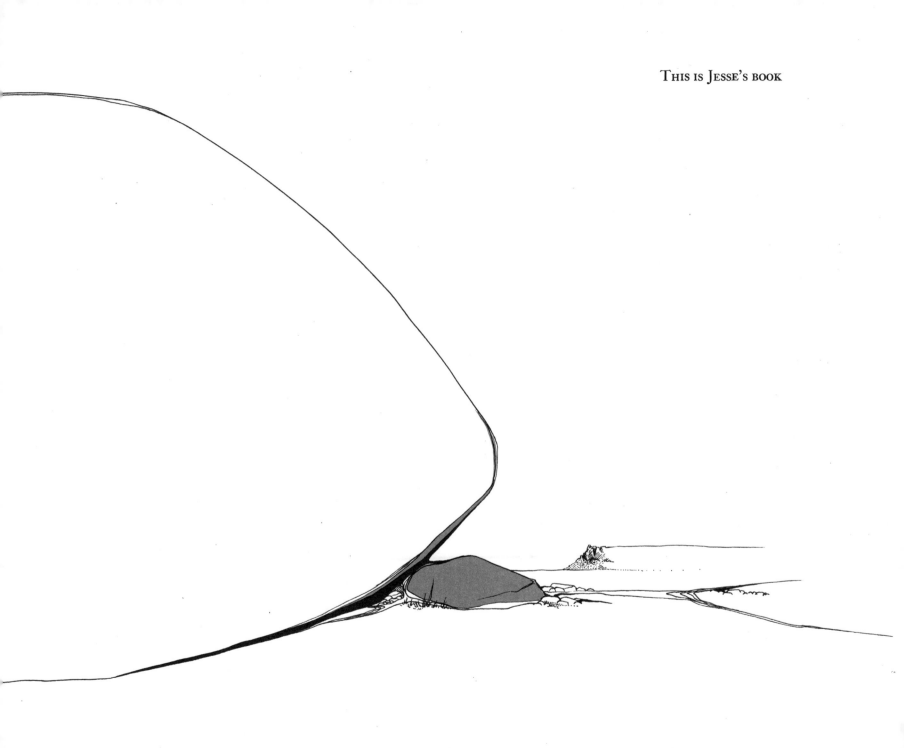

THIS IS JESSE'S BOOK

Everybody
needs
a rock.

I'm sorry for kids
who don't have
a rock
for a friend.

I'm sorry for kids
who only have
TRICYCLES
BICYCLES
HORSES
ELEPHANTS
GOLDFISH
THREE-ROOM PLAYHOUSES
FIRE ENGINES
WIND-UP DRAGONS
AND THINGS LIKE THAT —
if
they don't have
a
rock
for a friend.

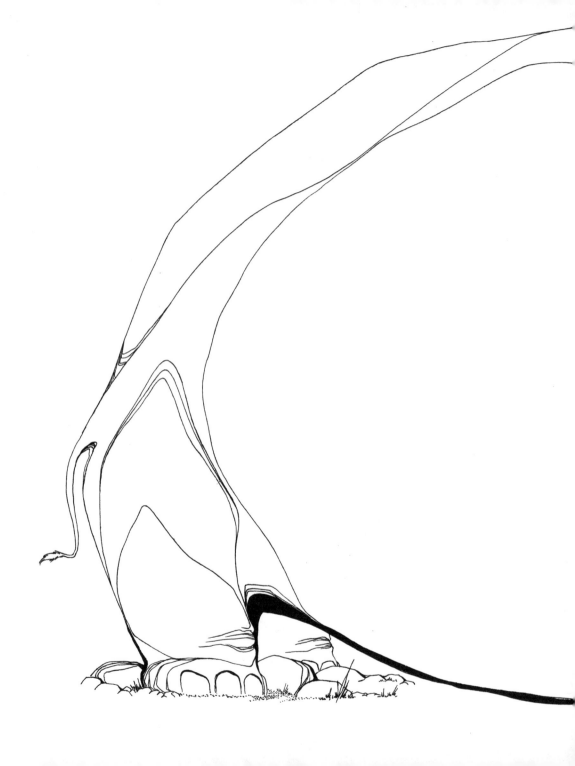

That's why
I'm giving them
my own
TEN RULES
for
finding
a
rock. . . .

Not
just
any rock.
I mean
a
special
rock
that you find
yourself
and keep
as long as
you can —
maybe
forever.

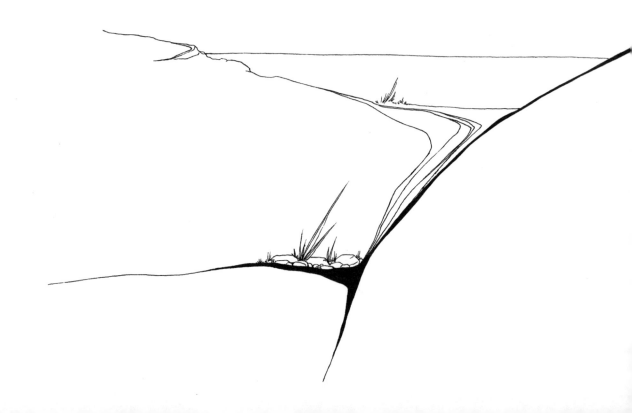

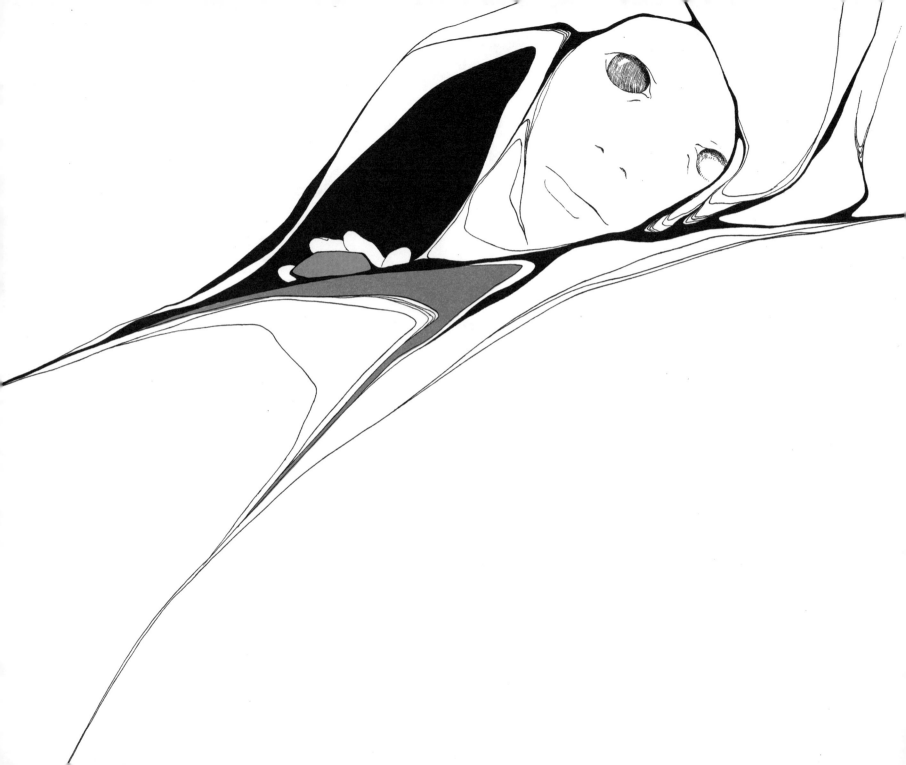

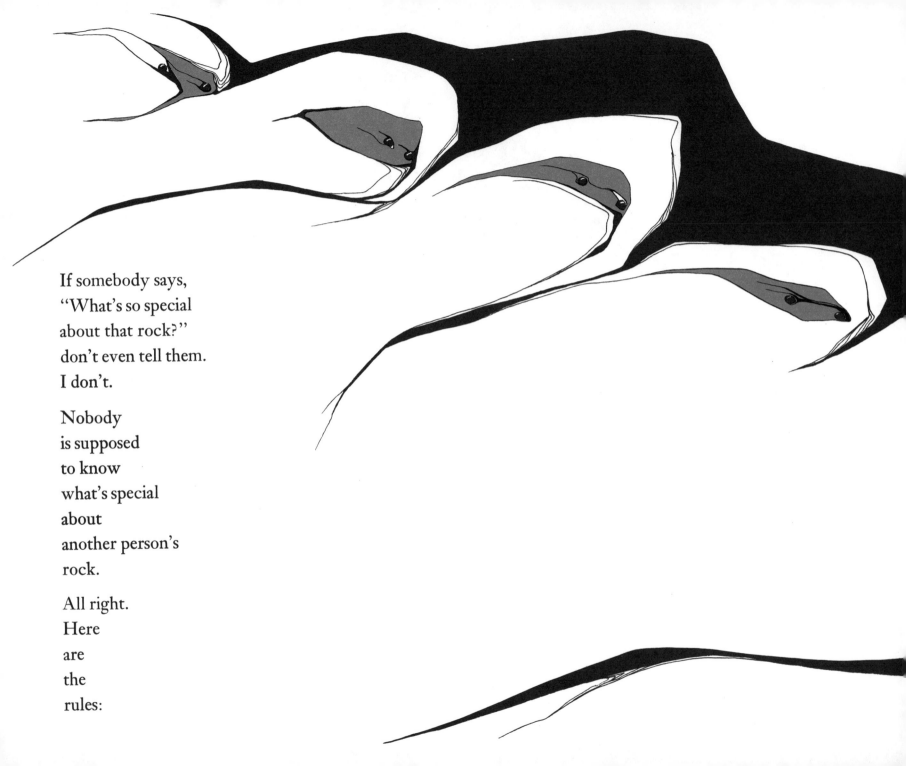

If somebody says,
"What's so special
about that rock?"
don't even tell them.
I don't.

Nobody
is supposed
to know
what's special
about
another person's
rock.

All right.
Here
are
the
rules:

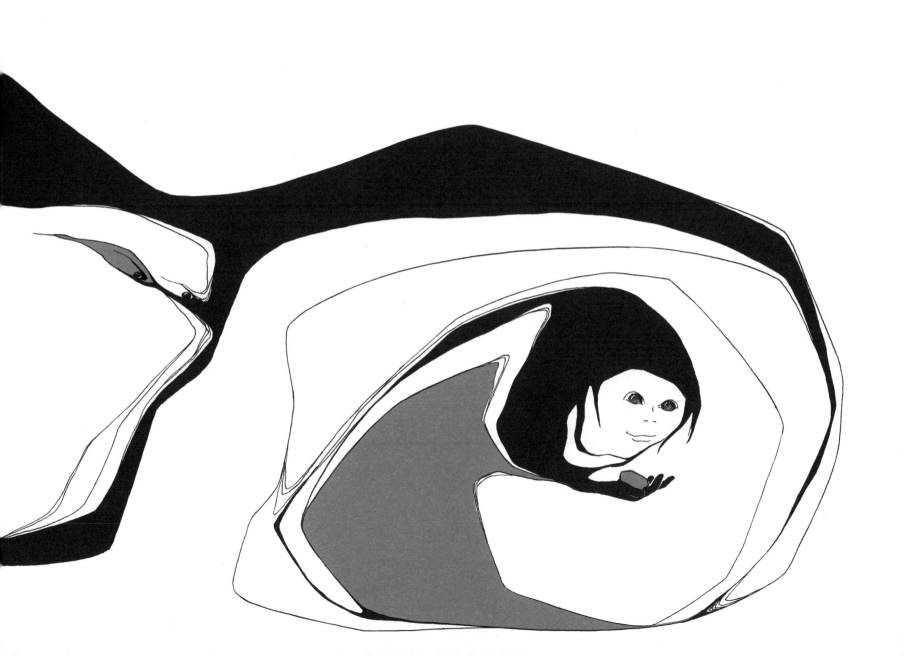

RULE NUMBER 1

If you can,
go to a mountain
made out of
nothing but
a hundred million
small
shiny
beautiful
roundish
rocks.

But if you can't,
anyplace will do.
Even an alley.
Even a sandy road.

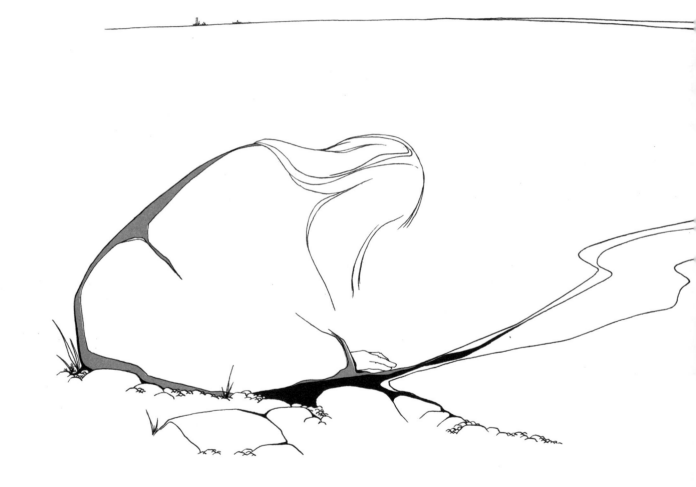

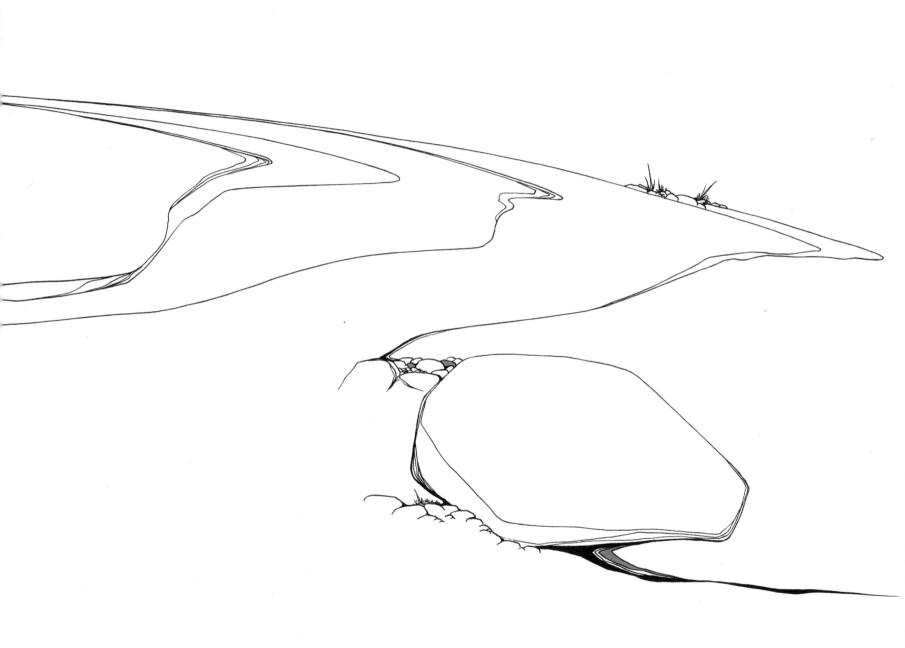

RULE NUMBER 2

When you are looking
at rocks
don't let
mothers or fathers
or sisters or brothers
or even best friends
talk
to you.
You should choose
a rock
when everything
is quiet.
Don't let dogs bark
at you
or bees buzz
at you.

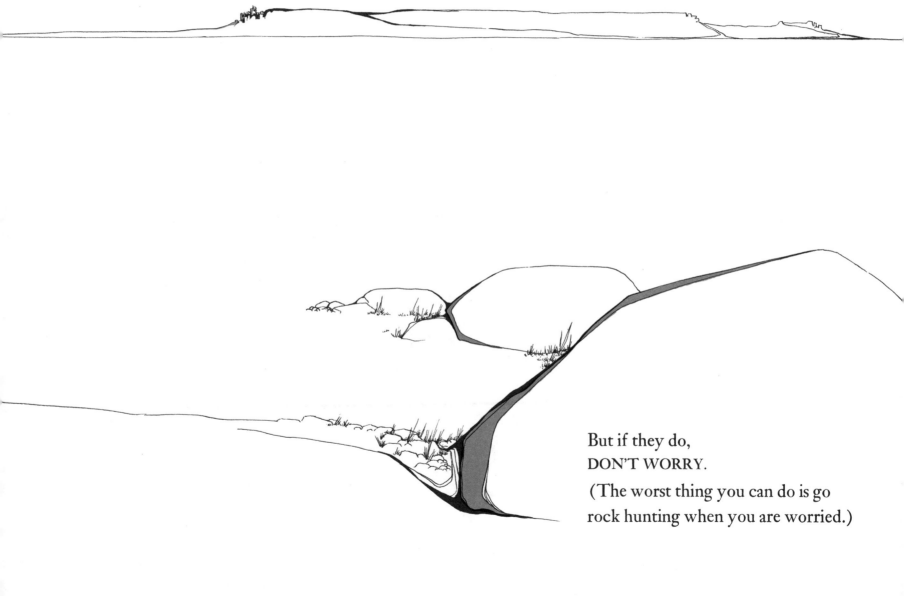

But if they do,
DON'T WORRY.

(The worst thing you can do is go
rock hunting when you are worried.)

RULE NUMBER 3

Bend over.
More.
Even more.
You may have to
sit
on the ground
with your head
almost
touching
the earth.
You have to look
a rock
right
in the eye.

Otherwise,
don't blame me
if you
can't find
a good one.

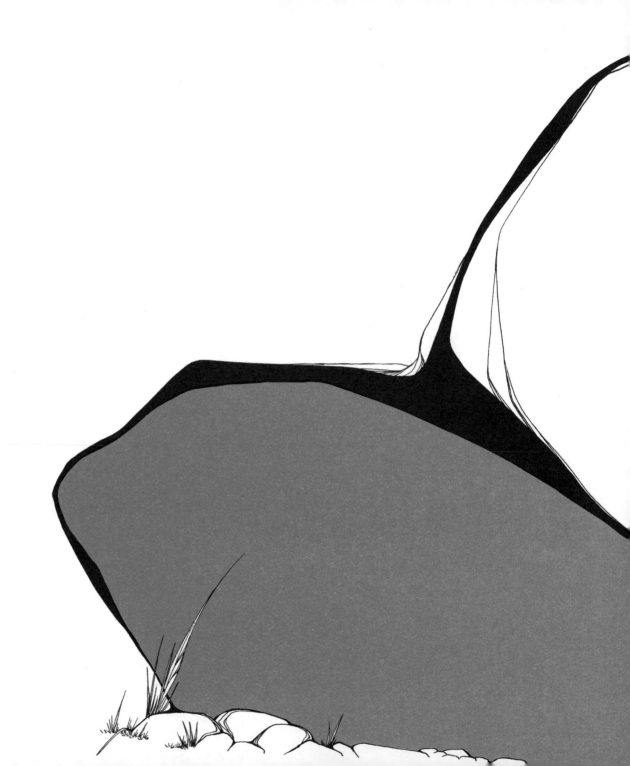

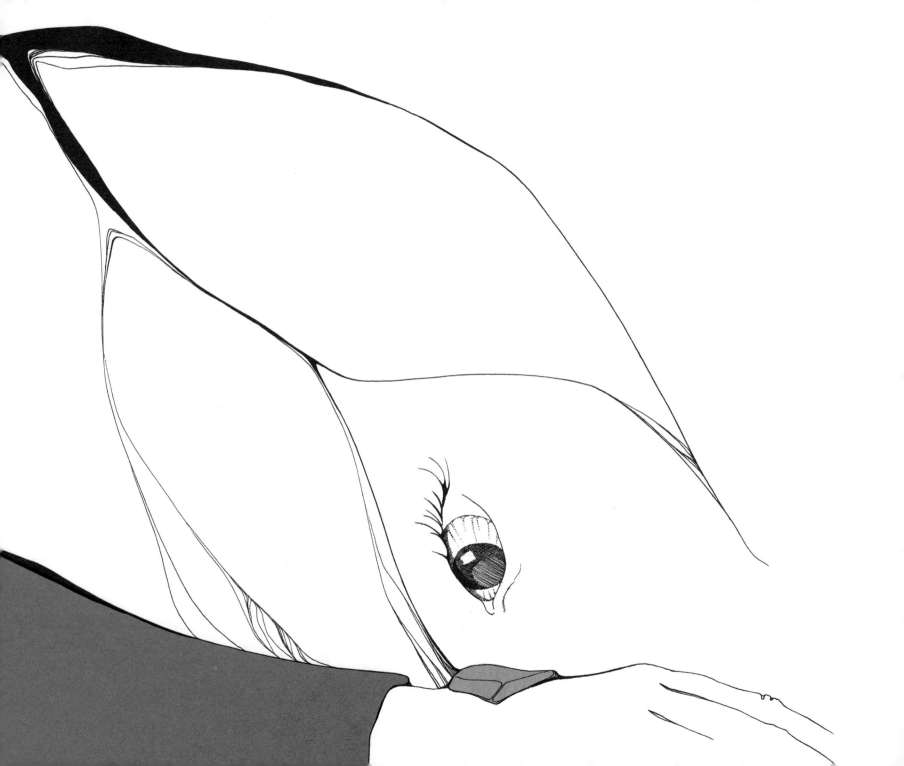

RULE NUMBER 4

Don't get a rock
that is
too big.
You'll
always
be sorry.
It won't fit
your hand
right
and it won't fit
your pocket.

A rock as big as
an apple
is too big.
A rock as big as
a horse
is
MUCH
too big.

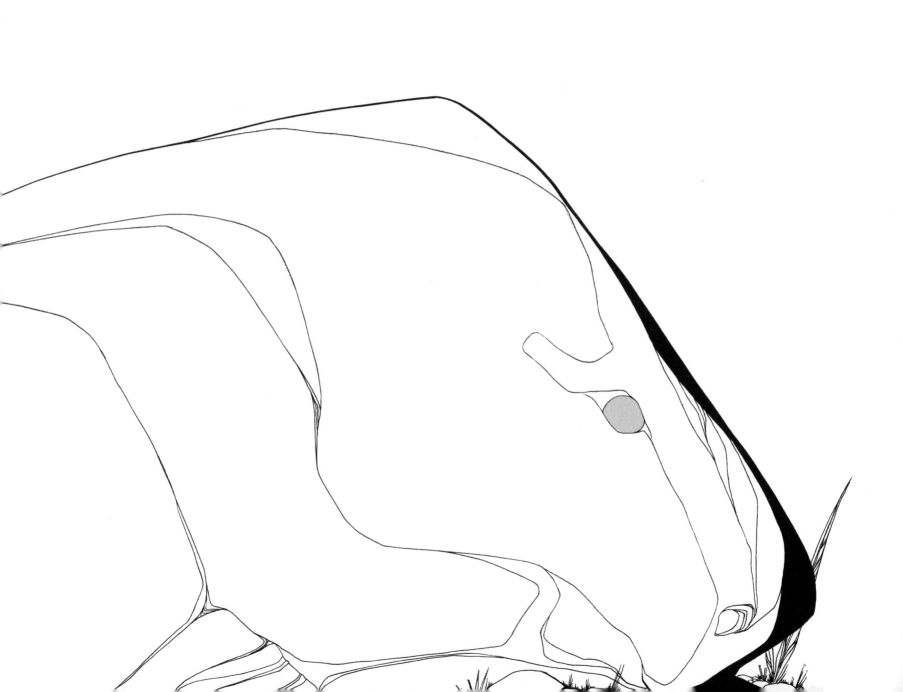

RULE NUMBER 5

Don't choose a rock
that is
too small.
It will only be
easy
to lose
or
a mouse
might eat it,
thinking
that it
is a seed.

(Believe me,
that happened
to a boy
in the state
of Arizona.)

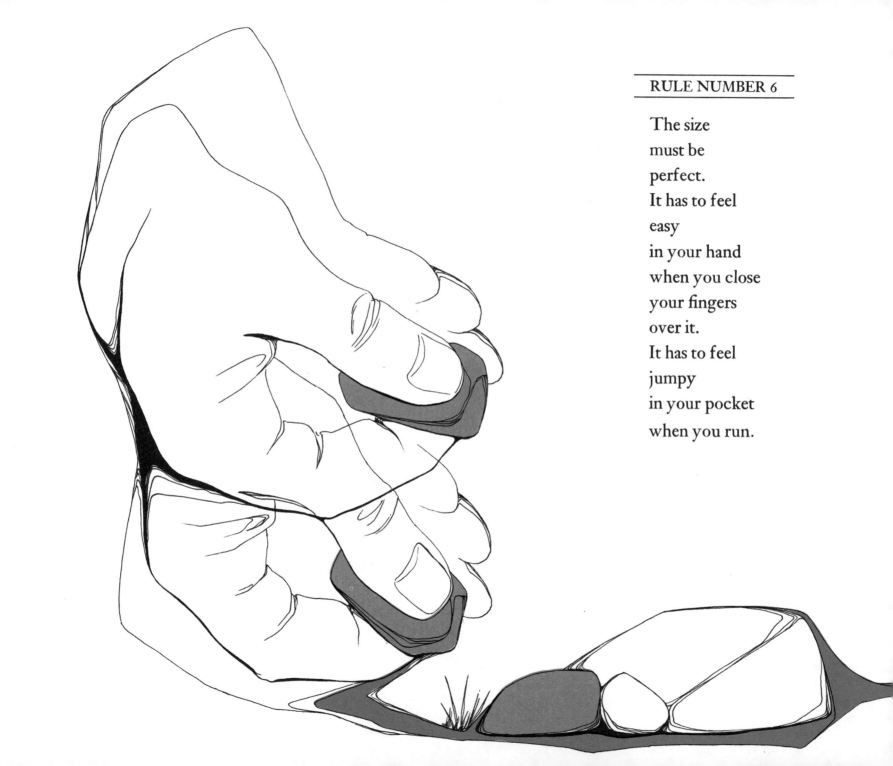

RULE NUMBER 6

The size
must be
perfect.
It has to feel
easy
in your hand
when you close
your fingers
over it.
It has to feel
jumpy
in your pocket
when you run.

Some people
touch
a rock
a thousand times
a day.
There aren't many things
that feel
as good as a rock —
if the rock
is
perfect.

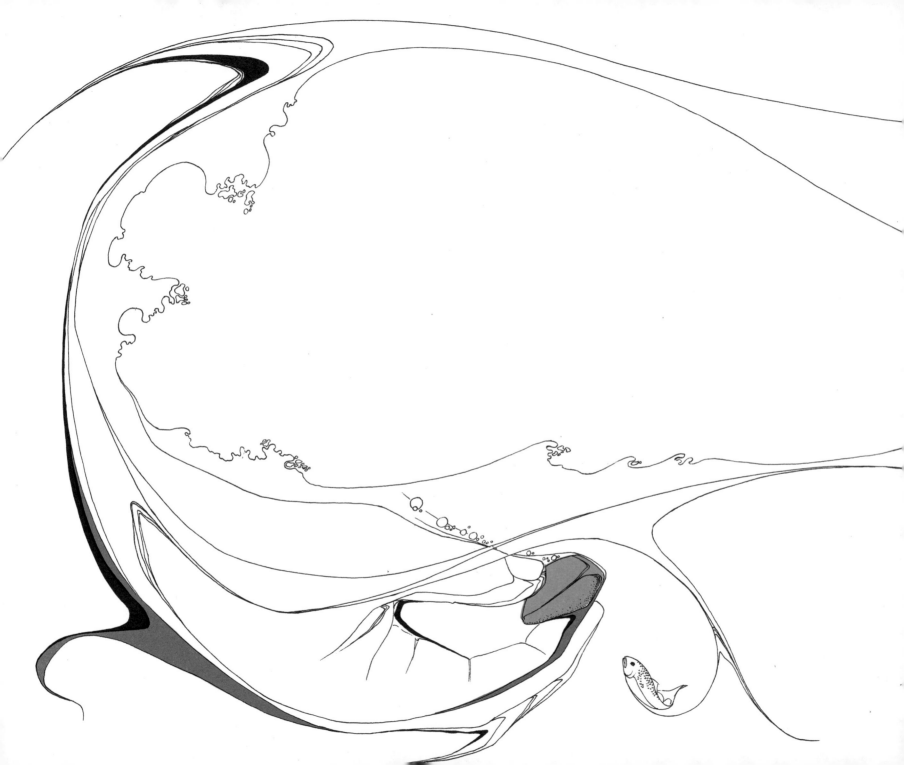

RULE NUMBER 7

Look for
the perfect
color.
That could be
a sort of
pinkish gray
with bits of
silvery shine in it.
Some rocks
that look brown
are really other
colors,
but
you only see them
when you squint
and when the sun
is right.

Another way
to see colors
is to dip
your rock
in a clear mountain stream —
if one is passing by.

The shape
of the rock
is up to you.
(There is a girl in Alaska
who only likes flat rocks.
Don't ask me why.
I like them lumpy.)

The thing to remember
about shapes
is this:
Any rock
looks good
with a hundred other rocks
around it on a hill.
But
if your rock
is going to be special
it should look good
by itself
in the bathtub.

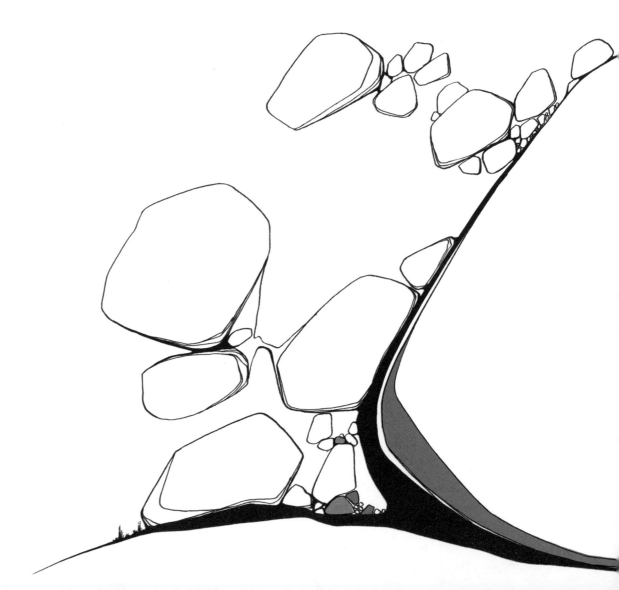

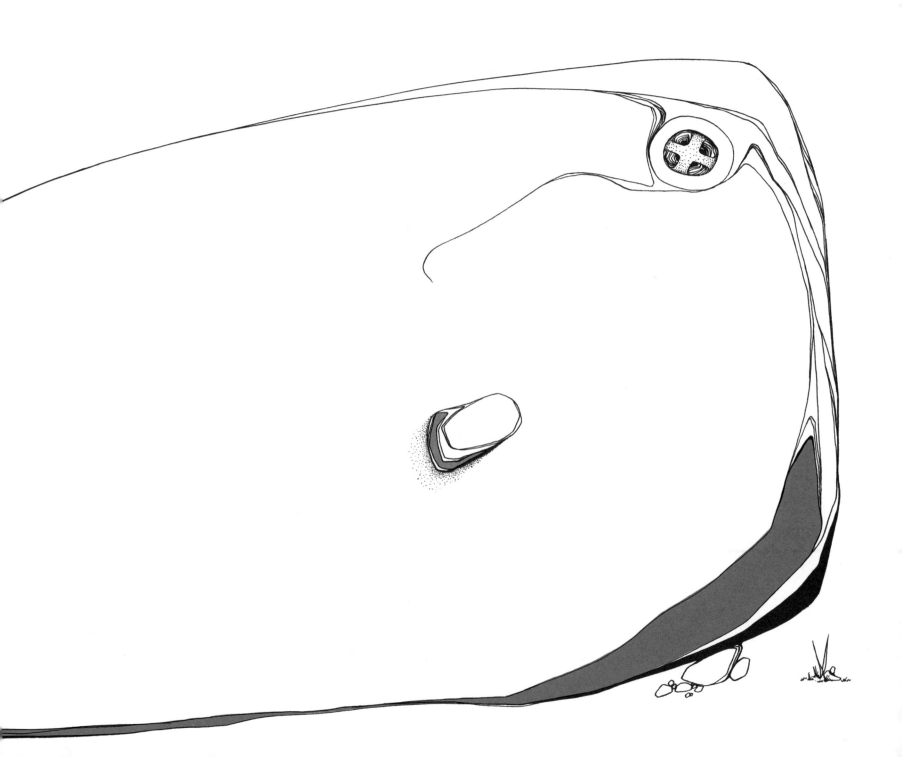

Always
sniff
a rock.
Rocks have
their own smells.
Some kids can tell
by sniffing
whether a rock
came from the middle
of the earth
or from an ocean
or from a mountain
where wind and sun
touched it
every day
for a million years.

You'll find out that grown-ups
can't tell these things.
Too bad for them.
They just can't smell as well
as kids can.

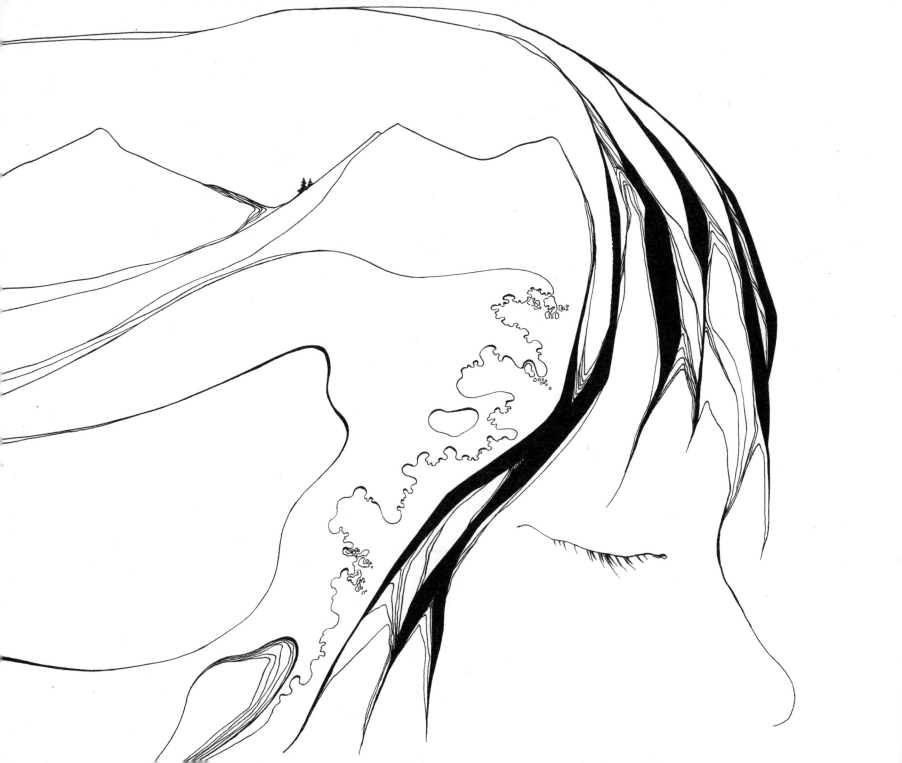

RULE NUMBER 10

Don't ask anybody
to help you choose.

I've seen
a lizard
pick one rock
out of
a desert full
of rocks
and go sit there
alone.
I've seen
a snail
pass up
twenty rocks
and spend all day
getting to
the one
it wanted.

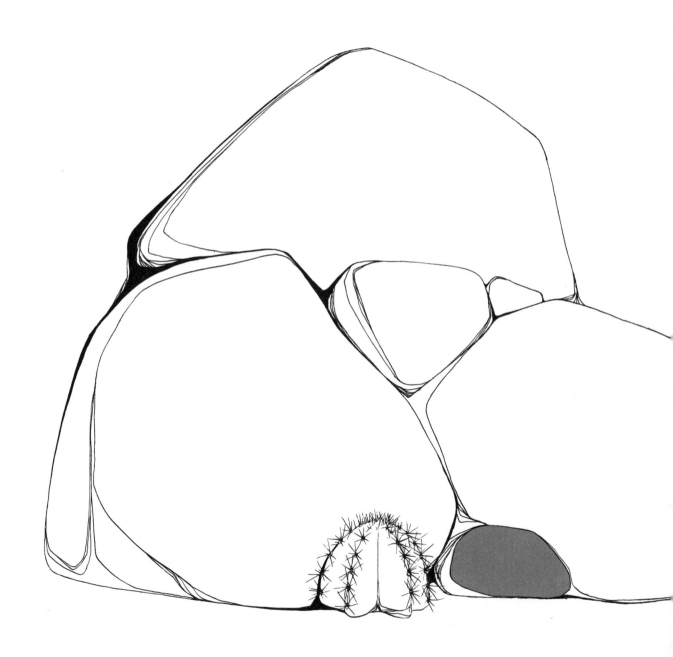

You have to
make up
your own mind.
You'll
know.

All right,
that's
ten rules.
If you think
of any more
write them down
yourself.
I'm going out
to play a game
that takes
just me
and one rock
to play.

I happen to have
a rock here in my hand . . .

200 easy dinners

200 easy dinners

hamlyn **all color**

Jo McAuley

An Hachette UK Company
www.hachette.co.uk

First published in Great Britain in 2008 by
Hamlyn, a division of Octopus Publishing Group Ltd,
2–4 Heron Quays, London E14 4JP
www.octopusbooksusa.com

Distributed in the U.S. and Canada by Octopus Books USA:
c/o Hachette Book Group USA
237 Park Avenue
New York NY 10017

ISBN: 978-0-600-61870-6

A CIP catalog record of this book is available from the
Library of Congress.

Printed and bound in China

2 3 4 5 6 7 8 9 10

People with known nut allergies should avoid recipes
containing nuts or nut derivatives, and vulnerable people
should avoid dishes containing raw or lightly cooked eggs.

Standard level spoon measurements are used in all recipes.

Ovens should be preheated to the specified temperature
—if using a fan-assisted oven, follow the manufacturer's
instructions for adjusting the time and the temperature.

Fresh herbs should be used unless otherwise stated.

Medium eggs should be used unless otherwise stated.

Some of the recipes in this book have previously appeared
in the following books published by Hamlyn:*Olive Cookbook*
by Jo McAuley; *Citrus* by Jo McAuley; and *Indoor Grilling*
by Jo McAuley

contents

introduction

introduction

Being passionate about food and wanting to cook needn't mean spending hours in a hot kitchen, slaving over the stove. No matter how much you enjoy cooking, there is so much else to do and so many other claims on your time that preparing and cooking food sometimes has to come last, and it's all too easy to reach for a ready-made, prepackaged meal from the supermarket shelves.

The recipes in this book show that cooking can be easy. Not all, but most of the recipes take less than 30 minutes to prepare from start to finish, and those that take longer are the kind of recipes you can generally leave to cook away gently so that they'll be ready once you have wound down from the stresses of the day. In general, the ingredients lists are short, the methods minimal, and the preparation and cooking times short. This is not to say that the dishes themselves fall below delicious—quite the opposite, in fact.

Experiment

The majority of the recipes serve four as a main course, but many of the salads, soups, and vegetarian options would make great appetizers, when, left as they are, they will comfortably feed eight people. Halve the quantities to serve two. If you are serving a dessert, choose something that can be made in advance, such as a sorbet, or that will cook while you are eating the first course.

Follow the recipes but feel free to alter the quantities or experiment with the choice of ingredients. Cooking should be fun, and even "easy" doesn't mean that you can't play around and adjust them according to taste.

Healthy eating

A healthy diet is usually a varied diet, and the recipes in this book will help you achieve that without too much hard work or stress. Remember that "easy" cooking doesn't have to mean reheating a ready-made microwave meal or eating junk food. Just because you don't have a great deal of time, there is no reason to miss out on essential vitamins and minerals and the nutrients that are found in

ingredients such as legumes and lentils. Cooking does not have to be long and complicated to ensure you are receiving all your nutritional needs.

The most important way to make sure that you are maintaining your intake of vitamins and minerals is to buy the freshest possible ingredients. We all know that we should aim for at least five daily portions of fruit and vegetables, but don't forget that frozen produce often has an equal, sometimes even a higher, nutritional value to fresh as long as it is processed immediately after picking.

Being prepared

We are told all the time how important it is to shop wisely. This is never more true than when you are aiming to cook simple, quick dishes, where each ingredient is of the utmost importance. For example, a fantastic olive oil or organic wild salmon fillet can make the difference between a dish that is merely acceptable and one that tastes wonderful. Many of the recipes in this book have one or two strong flavors, which serve to bring the dish to life. It's amazing how the zestiness of a lemon or the perfume of a few sage leaves can transform a meal. Fresh herbs, good-quality ingredients and a great combination of flavors and textures mean that easy cooking does not mean boring eating.

Don't feel guilty about making life a little easier and making the most of the great-quality, ready-made time-savers that are so readily available to us today. When you are shopping, look out for jars of pesto and tapenades, cooked rice, lentils, and legumes, deli-style roast vegetables. Look out, too, for jars of ready-minced garlic and ginger, which are now widely available in supermarkets and which mean that you can add the wonderful flavors without having to spend time peeling, crushing, and grating. Don't forget that you can also buy pre-cut strips of meat, such as beef or pork, which is perfect for stir-fries. Frozen pastry is essential for anyone wanting to cook easy pies or tarts: just remember to take it out of the freezer in good time to thaw before you start cooking.

Pantry essentials

One of the best ways of making life easy in the kitchen is to have a well-stocked pantry and freezer, so you need to buy just one or two items—fresh fish or meat or some seasonal vegetables—and combine them with staples such as rice and noodles and some well-flavored spices or ready-made sauces.

Legumes, lentils, & beans

Cans of precooked beans and lentils can be quickly heated through to make a simple meal substantial and filling. Experiment with different types. For example, cranberry beans are pretty and speckled when dried and light brown once cooked. Cannellini beans are a similar size to kidney beans but pale in color.

Puy lentils are small, round, flattish lentils, slate gray in color, and they are widely agreed to be the best of lentils because of their slightly peppery taste and the fact that they will hold their shape and slight bite during cooking, making them more robust than most lentils. They are available ready-cooked or dried in most good supermarkets.

Pasta, noodles, grains, & rice

Pasta takes little time to cook and can be used to accompany a wide range of dishes. Rice takes longer to cook, but it is possible to buy precooked rice. Cellophane, rice and udon noodles take just a few minutes to prepare and can be added to soups and stir-fries to create filling, nourishing dishes.

Less often used, but just as useful for the easy cook, is wild rice. It is actually a kind of grass and is very hard, so it needs to be cooked for longer than white rice—but it has a delicious, slightly nutty flavor. Wild rice tends to be more expensive than white and brown rices and so is often mixed with white rice to reduce the cost yet retain its taste.

You should also experiment with quinoa, a protein-rich grain that is light and tasty and which can be used as a side dish or part of a main course, or added to soups, salads, or appetizers and even desserts and cakes.

Polenta, an Italian staple made from cornmeal, takes about 40 minutes to cook from scratch, but it is also available in precooked form, which will only take a few minutes to prepare, or as firm polenta, which has been cooked and usually baked in rectangles so that it can be sliced and fried in oil.

Herbs & spices

Make sure your shelves are well stocked with spices and herbs. It is also easy to keep a few herbs—basil, parsley, and cilantro—growing on the kitchen windowsill, so that you can add a few freshly chopped leaves to garnish finished dishes.

Thai basil is very different from the more familiar herb we tend to use. It has dark green leaves and purplish stems and flowers, and its flavors are sweet, pungent, and slightly aniseed. It is used throughout Thailand and beyond in stir-fries and salads. It is possible to buy it fresh, and some good supermarkets also stock Thai basil in jars.

Most large supermarkets and specialty stores stock other prepared spices that will bring novel and interesting flavors to your easy dishes. Ras el hanout is a blend of up to 21 spices used in Middle Eastern and North African cooking. Chinese five spice combines equal parts of star anise, Szechwan pepper, fennel, ground cinnamon, and cloves. Garam masala is a blend of ground spices, popular in Indian cooking, that is generally used at the end of cooking, stirred in just before serving to round off the flavors of the dish.

Sumac is the ground version of berries grown and dried around the Mediterranean and is used frequently in Greek and Turkish cooking. It has a tart, sour lemon taste. If you cannot get hold of sumac, grated lemon zest can be used instead.

Sauces & pastes

If you like to experiment with Eastern dishes, you will probably already have jars of Thai red and green sauces and bottles of soy sauce on your shelves.

Some of the recipes in this book include teriyaki sauce. Of course, you can make your own by heating soy, mirin, sugar, and sake together and bubbling until thickened. Otherwise, buy it ready-made from any supermarket or Asian food store.

Tahini is a thick paste made from hulled, roasted sesame seeds, and it is a key ingredient in hummus. You will find tahini in most supermarkets or Middle Eastern food stores.

Harissa is a very hot, North African smoked chili pepper paste. It is widely used in Moroccan and Tunisian cooking and is often served with couscous or as condiment with grilled meats and fish.

meat

lima bean & bacon soup

Serves **4**
Preparation time **15 minutes**
Cooking time **24 minutes**

2 tablespoons **olive oil**
6 oz **bacon**, chopped
2 tablespoons **butter**
1 **onion**, chopped
2 **garlic cloves**, roughly
   chopped
2 **celery sticks**, chopped
1 **leek**, roughly chopped
3 cups hot **ham** or
   vegetable stock
13 oz can **lima beans**,
   drained and rinsed
2 large sprigs of **parsley**
3 sprigs of **thyme**
2 **bay leaves**
6 tablespoons **heavy cream**
salt and **pepper**

Heat 1 tablespoon of the oil in a large pan and fry the bacon until it is crisp and golden. Remove with a slotted spoon and set aside to drain on paper towels.

Melt the butter and remaining oil in the pan over a medium heat and cook the onion, garlic, celery, and leek, stirring frequently, for about 10 minutes or until soft and golden.

Add the stock and lima beans with the herbs and season to taste. Bring to a boil, then turn the heat down and simmer gently for about 10 minutes before removing from the heat. Remove the herbs and blend until smooth.

Stir in the cream, season to taste, and serve in large bowls, sprinkled with crispy bacon.

For smoked sausage & cranberry bean soup, replace the smoked bacon with 8 oz smoked pork sausage and use a 13 oz can of cranberry beans instead of the lima beans. Omit the cream.

14

pan-fried liver & bacon salad

Serves **4**
Preparation time **10 minutes**
Cooking time **8–12 minutes**

6 tablespoons **olive oil**
12 oz **calf's liver**, dusted with
   seasoned flour
8 oz cooked **new potatoes**,
   sliced
7 oz **bacon**, sliced
3 **shallots**, sliced
2 tablespoons **raspberry
   vinegar**
1 tablespoon **wholegrain
   mustard**
1 head **frisée**, leaves
   separated
salt and **pepper**

Heat 2 tablespoons of the oil in a skillet. Fry the
floured liver for 1–2 minutes on each side. Lift onto
paper towels and keep warm.

Add 1 tablespoon of the oil to the pan and fry the
potato slices, turning occasionally, for 4–5 minutes or
until crisp and golden. Lift onto paper towels and keep
warm with the liver.

Add 1 tablespoon of the oil to the pan and fry the
bacon for 2–3 minutes before adding the shallots.
Cook until soft and golden.

Mix together the raspberry vinegar, mustard, and
remaining oil.

Arrange the salad leaves on serving plates and pile on
the potatoes, bacon, and shallots. Slice the liver thinly
before arranging on each salad, drizzle over the
dressing and serve.

For chicken liver, mushroom, & bacon salad, omit
the calf's liver and start by frying the potatoes, as
above. When adding the shallots to the bacon, also
add 4 oz button mushrooms. Lastly, fry 12 oz diced
chicken livers. Arrange as above.

thai beef salad

Serves **4**

Preparation time **15 minutes**, plus standing

Cooking time **6−8 minutes**

2 lean sirloin **steaks**, about 5 oz each, trimmed

5 oz **baby corn**

1 large **cucumber**

1 small **red onion**, finely chopped

3 tablespoons chopped **cilantro**

4 tablespoons **rice wine vinegar**

4 tablespoons **sweet chili dipping sauce**

2 tablespoons **sesame seeds**, lightly toasted, to garnish

Put the steaks in a preheated hot griddle pan and cook for 3−4 minutes on each side. Allow to rest for 10−15 minutes, then slice the meat thinly.

Meanwhile, cook the corn in boiling water for 3−4 minutes or until tender. Refresh under cold water and drain well.

Slice the cucumber in half lengthwise, then scoop out and discard the seeds. Cut the cucumber into ¼ inch slices.

Put the beef, corn, cucumber, onion, and chopped cilantro in a large bowl. Stir in the vinegar and chili sauce and mix well. Garnish the salad with sesame seeds and serve.

For Thai tofu salad, omit the steaks and cube 1 lb firm tofu. Griddle for 2−3 minutes on each side until hot and golden. Mix with the other ingredients and garnish, as above.

italian tenderloin steak parcels

Serves **4**
Preparation time **10 minutes**
Cooking time **20 minutes**

1 tablespoon **olive oil**
4 **tenderloin steaks**, about
   5 oz each
8 large squares of **phyllo**
   pastry
⅔ cup **butter**, melted
4 oz **buffalo mozzarella**
   cheese, cut into 4 slices
2 teaspoons chopped
   marjoram
2 teaspoons chopped
   oregano
4 **sun-blushed tomatoes**,
   shredded
2 tablespoons finely grated
   Parmesan cheese
salt and **pepper**

Salad
3 cups **arugula**
4 oz **buffalo mozzarella**
   cheese, cubed
½ **red onion**, finely sliced
   (optional)
2 ripe **plum tomatoes**, sliced

Heat the oil in a hot skillet and sear the steaks for 2 minutes on each side (they will continue cooking in the oven). Remove and set aside.

Brush each sheet of pastry with melted butter and arrange 2 sheets on a work surface. Place a steak in the center of the pastry, followed by a slice of mozzarella, one-quarter of the herbs and sun-blushed tomato shreds. Season and bring up the sides of the pastry. Scrunch it together at the top to seal the steak into a parcel. Sprinkle over one-quarter of the grated Parmesan. Repeat with the remaining steaks.

Cook in a preheated oven, 425°F, for 15 minutes until the pastry is crisp and golden brown. Remove and allow to rest for 2–3 minutes.

Toss the salad ingredients together, season, and serve with the parcels.

For summertime chicken parcels, use 4 chicken breasts instead of the steaks—you will need to fry them for about 5 minutes on each side. For a stronger flavor, replace the toppings with either 4 oz sliced Gorgonzola, 3 tablespoons roughly chopped walnuts, and 2 tablespoons roughly chopped chives or 4 oz sliced firm goat cheese, 3 tablespoons black pitted olives, and 2 tablespoons shredded basil.

malay beef with peanut sauce

Serves **4**

Preparation time **10 minutes**

Cooking time **15 minutes**

1 lb sirloin **steak**, thinly sliced

1 tablespoon **vegetable oil**

Marinade

½ teaspoon **turmeric**

1 teaspoon **ground cumin**

½ teaspoon **fennel seeds**

1 **bay leaf**, finely shredded

½ teaspoon **ground cinnamon**

5 tablespoons **coconut cream**

Rice

1¼ cups **Thai jasmine rice**

¾ cup **coconut milk**

½ teaspoon **salt**

Peanut sauce

2 tablespoons **crunchy
  peanut butter**

¼ teaspoon **cayenne pepper**

1 tablespoon **light soy sauce**

½ cup **coconut cream**

½ teaspoon **superfine sugar**

Make the marinade by mixing together all the ingredients in a nonmetallic bowl. Add the beef, mix thoroughly, then thread the beef onto skewers and set aside to marinate.

Put the rice, coconut milk, salt, and 1 cup water in a rice cooker or a covered saucepan over a low heat. Cook for about 15 minutes until the rice is cooked and the liquid has been absorbed.

Meanwhile, add the ingredients for the peanut sauce to a small saucepan with 3 tablespoons water and heat gently, stirring.

Heat the oil in a large skillet and cook the beef skewers for about 5 minutes, turning so that each side is browned evenly. Serve immediately with the rice and peanut sauce.

For bean sprout & carrot salad to serve as an accompaniment, coarsely grate 4 carrots, roughly chop 4 scallions, and combine with 3 cups bean sprouts.

lamb chops with olive couscous

Serves **4**

Preparation time **25 minutes**, plus marinating

Cooking time **10–12 minutes**

6 **anchovy fillets in olive oil**, drained and chopped

2 tablespoons **black olive tapenade**

2–3 sprigs of **thyme**, leaves stripped and chopped

1 sprig of **rosemary**, leaves stripped and chopped

2 **bay leaves**, torn

2–3 **garlic cloves**, crushed

finely grated zest of 1 **lemon**

4 tablespoons **white wine**

½ cup **olive oil**

4 **lamb loin chops**, about 5 oz each

1⅔ cups **medium-grain couscous**

2 tablespoons **salted capers** or **capers in brine**, drained and rinsed

½ cup **spicy-marinated green olives**, chopped

2 cups **wild arugula leaves**, plus extra for serving

4 tablespoons **lemon juice**, plus extra for serving

salt and **pepper**

Mash the anchovies with a fork and stir them into a bowl with the tapenade. Add the herbs, garlic, and lemon zest, then pour in the wine and 4 tablespoons of the oil. Stir thoroughly, then rub the mixture into the lamb chops. Cover and leave at room temperature for about 1 hour.

Put the couscous into a heatproof bowl and stir in 2 tablespoons of the oil so that the grains are covered. Season with salt and pour over 1¾ cups boiling water. Allow to stand for 5–8 minutes until the grains are soft.

Season the lamb chops with pepper and cook them for about 2 minutes in a preheated hot griddle pan. Sprinkle with a little salt, then cook the other side for an additional 2 minutes. Transfer to a warm dish, cover with foil and allow to rest for 5 minutes.

Fluff up the couscous with a fork and gently fold in the capers, olives, and arugula. Sprinkle with the lemon juice, then heap the couscous onto warm plates. Arrange a lamb chop on each heap and spoon over the juices. Sprinkle with arugula leaves, drizzle with the remaining oil and an extra squeeze of lemon juice and serve immediately with lemon wedges.

For stir-fried lamb, heat 1½ tablespoons vegetable oil in a wok and cook 8 oz lamb tenderloin, thinly sliced, for a few minutes. Add 1 tablespoon each oyster sauce and Thai fish sauce, 1 crushed garlic clove, and 1 tablespoon finely sliced red chili and cook for an additional 2 minutes. Garnish with mint leaves.

sri lankan-style lamb curry

Serves **4**

Preparation time **10 minutes**

Cooking time **28–33 minutes**

1 lb **shoulder** or **leg of lamb**, diced

2 **potatoes**, peeled and cut into large chunks

4 tablespoons **olive oil**

13 oz can **chopped tomatoes**

salt and **pepper**

Curry paste

1 **onion**, grated

1 tablespoon finely chopped fresh **ginger root**

1 teaspoon finely chopped **garlic**

½ teaspoon **turmeric**

1 teaspoon **ground coriander**

½ teaspoon **ground cumin**

½ teaspoon **fennel seeds**

½ teaspoon **cumin seeds**

3 **cardamom pods**, lightly crushed

2 **green chilies**, finely chopped

2 inch **cinnamon stick**

2 **lemon grass stalks**, finely sliced

Make the curry paste by mixing together all the ingredients in a large bowl—for a milder curry remove the seeds from the chilies before chopping them finely. Add the lamb and potatoes and combine well.

Heat the oil in a heavy pan or casserole and tip in the meat and potatoes. Use a wooden spoon to stir-fry for 6–8 minutes. Pour in the chopped tomatoes and ⅔ cup water, bring to a boil and season well then allow to bubble gently for 20–25 minutes until the potatoes are cooked and the lamb is tender.

Serve accompanied with toasted naan bread and a bowl of Greek or whole milk yogurt, if desired.

For beef & potato curry, use 1 lb diced sirloin steak instead of the lamb. Prepare it in the same way as the lamb, then serve it with a generous sprinkling of chopped cilantro.

lamb with rosemary oil

Serves **4**

Preparation time **10 minutes**

Cooking time **10–20 minutes**

about 1½ lb **lamb loin roast**,
   trimmed of fat

4 **garlic cloves**, cut into slivers

a few small sprigs of
   rosemary

2 **red onions**, quartered

3 tablespoons **olive oil**

1 tablespoon chopped
   rosemary

salt and **pepper**

Make small incisions all over the lamb loin and insert the garlic slivers and rosemary sprigs.

Place the meat in a preheated hot griddle pan and cook, turning occasionally, until seared all over for about 10 minutes for rare or about 20 minutes for well done.

Add the onions halfway through the cooking time and char on the outside. Let the lamb rest for 5 minutes, then carve into slices.

Meanwhile, put the oil and rosemary in a mortar and crush with a pestle to release the flavors. Season with salt and pepper.

Spoon the rosemary oil over the lamb slices and serve at once with the fried onions.

Serve with fresh pasta, lightly tossed in oil, and Parmesan shavings.

For lamb chops with garlic & herbs, cut 4 garlic cloves into slivers and insert into incisions in 8 lamb chops. Place each chop on a square of foil and divide ¼ cup butter, 3 tablespoons lemon juice, and 1 tablespoon each dried oregano and dried mint among them. Season and fold the foil to encase the meat. Cook in a preheated oven, 350°F, for 1½–2 hours.

taverna-style broiled lamb with feta

Serves **4**
Preparation time **8 minutes**
Cooking time **6–8 minutes**

1 lb leg or **shoulder of lamb**, diced

Marinade
2 tablespoons chopped **oregano**
1 tablespoon chopped **rosemary**
grated zest of 1 **lemon**
2 tablespoons **olive oil**
salt and **pepper**

Feta salad
8 oz **feta cheese**, sliced
1 tablespoon chopped **oregano**
2 tablespoons chopped **parsley**
grated zest and juice of 1 **lemon**
½ small **red onion**, finely sliced
3 tablespoons **olive oil**

Mix together the marinade ingredients in a non-metallic bowl, add the lamb and mix to coat thoroughly. Thread the meat onto 4 skewers.

Arrange the sliced feta on a large serving dish and sprinkle with the herbs, lemon zest, and sliced onion. Drizzle over the lemon juice and oil and season with salt and pepper.

Cook the lamb skewers under a preheated hot broiler or in a griddle pan for about 6–8 minutes, turning frequently until browned and almost cooked through. Remove from heat and allow to rest for 1–2 minutes.

Serve the lamb, with any pan juices poured over, with the salad and accompanied with plenty of crusty bread, if desired.

For pork with red cabbage, replace the lamb with the same quantity of lean, boneless pork. Marinate and cook the pork as above. Replace the feta with 2 cups finely chopped red cabbage. Omit the oregano and swap the lemon for an orange. Mix the ingredients together and marinate for 5 minutes before serving.

fragrant lamb cutlets

Serves **4**
Preparation time **5 minutes**,
   plus marinating
Cooking time **15 minutes**

12 **lamb cutlets**
4 **sweet potatoes**, baked
   in their skins
salt and **pepper**
arugula leaves, to serve

Marinade
finely grated zest and juice
   of ½ **lemon**
2 **garlic cloves**, crushed
2 tablespoons **olive oil**, plus
   extra for brushing
4 sprigs of **rosemary**, finely
   chopped
4 **anchovy fillets in olive oil**,
   drained and finely chopped
2 tablespoons **lemon cordial**

Mix together all the marinade ingredients in a non-metallic bowl, then add the lamb cutlets. Season to taste with salt and pepper, turn the cutlets to coat, and set aside for 15 minutes to marinate.

Cook the cutlets under a preheated hot broiler for 3–5 minutes on each side or until slightly charred and cooked through. Keep warm and allow to rest.

Meanwhile, cut the baked sweet potatoes into quarters, scoop out some of the flesh and brush the skins with oil. Season to taste with salt and pepper and cook for about 15 minutes under the broiler until crisp. Serve with the lamb cutlets and arugula leaves.

For pork patties with sweet potato slices, mix 1 lb ground pork with the marinade ingredients, omitting the anchovies. Using your hands, form the pork mixture into little patties and cook under a hot broiler for 5–6 minutes on each side until browned and cooked through. Serve with sweet potato skins and arugula leaves, as above.

pork tenderloin with mushrooms

Serves **4**
Preparation time **15 minutes**
Cooking time **15–17 minutes**

4 tablespoons **olive oil**
1 lb **pork tenderloin**, sliced
    into ¼ inch disks
10 oz **mushrooms**, trimmed
    and cut into chunks
1 **lemon**
1¼ cups **sour cream**
2 sprigs of **tarragon**, leaves
    stripped
salt and **pepper**

Heat 2 tablespoons of the oil in a skillet over a medium-high heat and fry the pork slices for 3–4 minutes, turning once so that they are browned on both sides. Remove with a slotted spoon.

Add the remaining oil to the pan, tip in the mushrooms and cook for 3–4 minutes, stirring occasionally, until softened and golden.

Cut half of the lemon into slices and add to the pan to brown a little on each side, then remove and set aside.

Return the pork to the pan, add the sour cream and tarragon and pour in the juice from the remaining lemon. Season well, bring to a boil, then reduce the heat and allow to bubble gently for 5 minutes. Add the prepared lemon slices at the last minute and gently stir through.

Serve the pork with white rice or crispy potato wedges.

For couscous with petit pois to serve as an accompaniment, soak 1½ cups couscous in 1¾ cups just-boiled water or vegetable stock and leave for 5–8 minutes until soft. Fluff up the couscous with a fork and season. Boil 1 cup frozen petit pois for 3 minutes, drain, then mix them with the couscous. Before serving, add a handful of chopped chives, a few pieces of butter and season with black pepper.

pork in cider with pappardelle

Serves **4**

Preparation time **8 minutes**

Cooking time **20 minutes**

⅛ cup **dried wild mushrooms**

3 tablespoons **olive oil**

13 oz boneless **pork loin steaks**

5 oz **bacon**, sliced

8 **shallots**, quartered

1¼ cups **hard cider**

½ cup **cider vinegar**

2 sprigs of **thyme**

1 **bay leaf**, torn

13 oz fresh **pappardelle** or thick ribbon pasta

¾ cup **sour cream**

salt and **pepper**

Soak the dried mushrooms for 5–10 minutes in 6 tablespoons boiling water.

Meanwhile, heat the oil in a large skillet over a medium heat and fry the pork and bacon for approximately 3 minutes until browned. Add the shallots and continue frying for an additional 2–3 minutes until golden and beginning to soften.

Pour in the hard cider and cider vinegar and add the mushrooms and soaking liquid. Stir in the herbs and season well. Bring to a boil, then reduce the heat, cover and allow to bubble gently for 10–12 minutes until the shallots are soft.

Meanwhile, cook the pasta in lightly salted boiling water for 3 minutes or according to the instructions on the package. Drain and transfer to serving dishes.

Stir the sour cream into the pork, increase the heat briefly and then place the meat on the pasta and spoon over the sauce. Serve immediately.

For venison in red wine, substitute the pork with 4 venison steaks cut into strips and replace the cider with red wine. Omit the cider vinegar. Serve as above.

crispy prosciutto parcels

Serves **4**
Preparation time **10 minutes**
Cooking time **4 minutes**

8 slices of **prosciutto**
4 oz creamy **blue cheese**,
  such as Roquefort, St Agur,
  dolcelatte, or Gorgonzola,
  thinly sliced
1 teaspoon chopped **thyme
  leaves**
1 **pear**, peeled, cored, and
  diced
¼ cup **walnuts**, chopped

To serve
watercress leaves tossed in
  olive oil and **balsamic
  vinegar**
1 **pear**, peeled, cored, and
  sliced

Put a slice of prosciutto on a cutting board and then put a second slice across it to form a cross shape.

Arrange one-quarter of the cheese slices in the center, sprinkle with some thyme and top with one-quarter of the diced pear.

Add one-quarter of the walnuts, then fold over the sides of the ham to form a neat parcel. Repeat this process to make 4 parcels.

Transfer the parcels to a foil-lined broiler pan and cook under a preheated hot broiler for about 2 minutes on each side until the ham is crisp and the cheese is beginning to ooze out of the sides.

Serve the parcels immediately with the dressed watercress leaves and slices of pear.

For figs with prosciutto, quarter 8 fresh figs, leaving them attached at the base. Mix 1 teaspoon Dijon mustard with ½ cup ricotta cheese, season to taste and spoon over the figs. Divide 3 oz prosciutto, cut into strips, among them and drizzle over 2 tablespoons balsamic vinegar.

pork chops with lemon & thyme

Serves **4**
Preparation time **20 minutes**
Cooking time **28–30 minutes**

finely grated zest of **1 lemon**
1 tablespoon chopped **thyme**
2 tablespoons **olive oil**
2 **garlic cloves**, crushed
4 **pork chops**, about 7 oz
   each
2 lb **floury potatoes**, peeled
   and quartered
¾ cup **heavy cream**
¼ cup **butter**
salt and **pepper**
thyme, leaves or flowers,
   to garnish

Mix together the lemon zest, thyme, oil, garlic, and plenty of pepper and rub the mixture over the pork chops. Set aside.

Meanwhile, cook the potatoes in lightly salted boiling water for about 20 minutes or until soft. Drain, return to the pan and mash. Add the cream, butter, and seasoning and use an electric hand-held beater to beat until smooth.

Heat a dry skillet over a medium-high heat and cook the pork chops for 4–5 minutes on each side, depending on their thickness, until cooked and golden.

Remove the pork from the heat and allow to rest for 1–2 minutes before serving garnished with a few thyme leaves or flowers and accompanied by the fluffy mash.

For spinach & Parmesan mash instead of plain mash, cook, drain, and chop 1 lb spinach. Mash the potatoes with butter and milk (omit the cream) and stir in the spinach and ½ cup freshly grated Parmesan.

pork with eggplant & noodles

Serves **4**

Preparation time **15 minutes**

Cooking time **15 minutes**

1 lb **ground pork**

8 oz **thick, flat rice noodles**

about 3 tablespoons
  vegetable or **peanut oil**

1 large **eggplant**, cut into
  ½ inch dice

2 tablespoons **cilantro leaves**,
  plus extra to garnish

Marinade

1 tablespoon **dark soy sauce**

3 tablespoons **light soy
  sauce**, plus extra to serve
  (optional)

1 tablespoon **cornstarch**

1 teaspoon **honey**

1 tablespoon **chili paste**

2 teaspoons finely chopped
  garlic

1 tablespoon finely chopped
  ginger root

Make the marinade by mixing together all the ingredients in a nonmetallic bowl. Add the pork and combine thoroughly until the liquid has been absorbed. Set aside.

Cook the noodles in boiling water for 2–3 minutes or according to the instructions on the package. Drain.

Heat the oil until smoking in a large wok or skillet. Carefully stir-fry the eggplant until golden and soft. Remove with a slotted spoon and leave to drain on paper towels.

Add more oil to the pan if necessary and stir-fry the pork until browned and cooked through. Pour in 5 tablespoons water and allow to gently bubble. Return the eggplant to the wok and heat through, then add the cilantro leaves.

Serve the pork and eggplant piled on top of the noodles and with a sprinkling of cilantro leaves and some extra light soy sauce, if desired.

For ground steak with okra & rice, cook 1¼ cups rice instead of noodles and substitute the ground pork with the same quantity of ground steak. Replace the eggplant with 7 oz okra, sliced into ½ inch pieces and fry for 5 minutes. Serve as above.

quick beef stroganoff

Serves **4**
Preparation time **10 minutes**
Cooking time **15 minutes**

2 tablespoons **paprika**
1 tablespoon **all-purpose flour**
1 lb sliced **beef sirloin**
1½ cups **long-grain white rice**
2 tablespoons **butter**
4 tablespoons **vegetable** or **sunflower oil**
1 large **onion**, thinly sliced
8 oz **chestnut mushrooms**, trimmed and sliced
1¼ cups **sour cream**
salt and **pepper**
1 tablespoon chopped **curly parsley**, to garnish

Mix together the paprika and flour in a large bowl, add the beef and turn to coat.

Cook the rice in lightly salted boiling water for 13 minutes until cooked but firm. Drain, set aside and keep warm.

Meanwhile, melt the butter and 2 tablespoons of the oil in a large skillet and cook the onion for about 6 minutes or until soft. Add the mushrooms and cook for an additional 5 minutes or until soft. Remove with a slotted spoon and set aside.

Add the remaining oil to the pan, increase the heat to high and add the beef. Fry until browned all over, then reduce the heat. Return the onion mixture to the pan along with the sour cream; bring to a boil, then reduce the heat and allow to bubble gently for 1–2 minutes. Season well.

Serve immediately with the cooked rice and a sprinkling of chopped parsley.

For mushroom & red pepper Stroganoff, omit the beef, increase the quantity of chestnut mushrooms to 1 lb and add 2 thinly sliced red bell peppers. Cook the mushrooms with the onion until they have reduced and the onion is soft. Remove the mixture from the pan. Cook the peppers until tender. Return the onion mixture to the pan, as above. Sprinkle with pine nuts to serve.

44

pork & peppercorn tagliatelle

Serves **4**

Preparation time **10 minutes**

Cooking time **20 minutes**

12 oz dried **tagliatelle verde** or similar

2 tablespoons **olive oil**

1 lb **pork tenderloin**, sliced

1 **onion**, finely chopped

1 large **garlic clove**, chopped

2 tablespoons **brandy**

5 tablespoons **white wine**

2 tablespoons **raisins** soaked in 3 tablespoons warm **apple juice**

1 teaspoon chopped **rosemary**

1½ tablespoons **green peppercorns in brine**, drained and chopped

3 **juniper berries** (optional)

1 cup **light cream**

salt and **pepper**

Cook the pasta in lightly salted boiling water according to the instructions on the package.

Meanwhile, heat the oil in a large skillet and brown the pork slices for 2 minutes, turning once. Remove with a slotted spoon and set aside. Add the onion to the pan and cook for about 5 minutes before adding the garlic. Cook for an additional minute until softened.

Pour in the brandy, wine, raisins and apple juice, rosemary, green peppercorns, and juniper berries (if used), bring to a boil and bubble over high heat for 1–2 minutes. Reduce the heat, stir in the cream, and simmer gently for 5 minutes.

Return the pork to the pan and stir for 3–5 minutes, or until cooked through and tender. Turn the heat off. Toss through the prepared pasta and serve.

For pork & sun-dried tomato tagliatelle, replace the raisins with chopped sun-dried tomatoes. There is no need to soak them in the apple juice, but don't omit it altogether: just add it at the same time as the tomatoes.

pepper-crusted loin of venison

Serves **4**

Preparation time **10 minutes**

Cooking time **up to
45 minutes**

1½ lb **loin of venison**, cut
from the haunch

¾ cup **mixed peppercorns**,
crushed

2 tablespoons **juniper
berries**, crushed

1 **egg white**, lightly beaten

salt and **pepper**

Make sure that the venison fits into your broiler pan;
if necessary, cut the loin in half to fit.

Mix together the peppercorns, juniper berries, and
some salt in a large, shallow dish. Dip the venison in
the egg white, then roll it in the peppercorn mixture,
covering it evenly all over.

Cook the venison under a preheated hot broiler for
4 minutes on each of the four sides, turning it carefully
so that the crust stays intact. Transfer the loin to a
lightly greased roasting pan and cook in a preheated
oven, 400°F, for another 15 minutes for rare and up to
30 minutes for well done (the time will depend on the
thickness of the loin of venison).

Allow the venison to rest for a few minutes, then slice
it thickly and serve with green beans, redcurrant jelly,
and finely sliced sweet potato chips.

For Chinese-style venison steaks with bok choy,
omit the peppercorns and juniper berries and replace
the loin of venison with four 4 x 6 oz venison steaks.
Make a marinade by mixing together 3 tablespoons
soy sauce, 1 tablespoon each finely grated fresh
ginger root, oyster sauce, and rice wine, 2 crushed
garlic cloves and 2 tablespoons peanut oil. Marinate
for up to an hour, then griddle for 3–4 minutes on
each side. Serve with noodles and bok choy.

chorizo & smoked paprika penne

Serves **4**
Preparation time **15 minutes**
Cooking time **26 minutes**

1 tablespoon **olive oil**
7 oz **chorizo sausage**, diced
1 **onion**, chopped
2 **garlic cloves**, chopped
1 teaspoon **hot smoked
  paprika**
1 tablespoon **capers**
1 teaspoon **dried oregano**
1 teaspoon finely grated
  lemon zest
pinch of **superfine sugar**
5 oz **roasted red sweet
  pepper**, sliced
1 lb 10 oz can **chopped
  tomatoes**
12 oz dried **penne**
salt and **pepper**

To serve
chili oil (optional)
4 tablespoons grated
  Parmesan cheese

Heat the oil in a large pan and fry the chorizo for 2 minutes until golden. Add the onion and garlic and cook for about 5 minutes or until soft and golden.

Stir in the paprika and cook for an additional minute, then add the capers, oregano, lemon zest, sugar, sweet pepper, and tomatoes. Bring to a boil, then reduce the heat and simmer gently for 15 minutes.

Meanwhile, cook the penne in lightly salted boiling water according to the instructions on the package.

Drain the pasta and stir it into the chorizo sauce. Serve immediately with a drizzle of chili oil (if used) and the freshly grated Parmesan.

For garlic, oregano, & Parmesan toasts, to serve as an accompaniment, split a ciabatta loaf in half lengthwise and then cut each length in half. Mix 1 crushed garlic clove with 1 teaspoon dried oregano and 2 tablespoons olive oil. Drizzle over the ciabatta and sprinkle each piece with 1 teaspoon finely grated Parmesan. Place under a hot broiler for 3–4 minutes until toasted and golden.

tartiflette-style pizza

Serves **4**

Preparation time **20 minutes**, plus resting

Cooking time **23–25 minutes**

10 oz **pizza base mix**

2 tablespoons **butter**

1 tablespoon **olive oil**

7 oz **bacon lardons** or **smoky bacon bits**

2 **onions**, sliced

1 **garlic clove**, chopped

¾ cup **sour cream**

8 oz cooked **potatoes**, thinly sliced

8 oz **Reblochon cheese**, sliced

Make the pizza base according to the instructions on the package. Form the dough into 4 balls and roll them out into ovals. Cover lightly with oiled plastic wrap and leave in a warm place.

Melt the butter and olive oil in a large skillet and fry the bacon for 3–4 minutes or until cooked. Add the onions and garlic and fry gently for 5–6 minutes or until soft and golden.

Spread 1 tablespoon of the sour cream over each pizza base. Top with slices of potato, some of the bacon and onion mixture, and 2–3 slices of Reblochon. Cook in a preheated oven, 425°F, for 15 minutes until bubbling and golden.

Serve immediately with an extra dollop of the remaining sour cream on top, if desired.

For artichoke heart & dolcelatte pizza, replace the potatoes with 2 x 15 oz cans of artichoke hearts, drained and halved. Top with sliced dolcelatte.

poultry

lime, ginger, & cilantro chicken

Serves **4**

Preparation time
5–10 minutes

Cooking time **50 minutes**

3 **limes**

½ inch cube **fresh ginger root**, peeled and finely grated

4 tablespoons finely chopped **cilantro**, plus extra leaves to serve

2 teaspoons **vegetable oil**

4 **chicken legs**

1½ cups **Thai jasmine rice**

salt

Finely grate the zest of 2 of the limes and halve these limes. Mix the zest with the ginger and cilantro in a nonmetallic bowl and stir in 1 teaspoon of the oil to make a rough paste.

Carefully lift the skin from the chicken legs and push under the ginger paste. Pull the skin back into place, then cut 3–4 slashes in the thickest parts of the legs and brush with the remaining oil.

Put the legs in a roasting pan, flesh-side down, with the halved limes and cook in a preheated oven, 425°F, for 45–50 minutes, basting occasionally. The legs are cooked when the meat comes away from the bone and the juices run clear.

Meanwhile, put the rice in a pan with 1¾ cups cold water, cover with a tight-fitting lid, and cook over a medium-low heat for 10 minutes until the water has been absorbed and the rice is almost cooked. Set aside somewhere warm until the chicken has finished cooking.

Spoon the rice into small bowls to mold, then turn it onto serving plates. Add the chicken legs, squeeze over the roasted lime, and sprinkle with cilantro leaves. Serve immediately with the remaining lime, cut into wedges.

For Mediterranean chicken, replace the ginger paste with a red pesto made by blending 6 sun-dried tomatoes, 1 tablespoon pine nuts, ½ clove chopped garlic, 1 tablespoon chopped basil, 1 teaspoon grated lemon zest, 1 tablespoon lemon juice, 3 tablespoons olive oil, and 1 tablespoon grated Parmesan cheese.

asian steamed-chicken salad

Serves **4**

Preparation time **10 minutes, plus cooling**

Cooking time **8–10 minutes**

4 boneless, skinless **chicken breasts**, about 5 oz each

½ small **Chinese cabbage**, finely shredded

1 large **carrot**, grated

3 cups **bean sprouts**

small bunch of **cilantro**, finely chopped

small bunch of **mint**, finely chopped

1 **red chili**, seeded and finely sliced (optional)

Dressing

½ cup **sunflower oil**

juice of 2 **limes**

1½ tablespoons **Thai fish sauce**

3 tablespoons **light soy sauce**

1 tablespoon finely chopped fresh **ginger root**

Put the chicken breasts in a bamboo or other steamer set over a large pan of simmering water. Cover and allow to steam for about 8 minutes or until the chicken is cooked through. Alternatively, poach the chicken for 8–10 minutes until the meat is cooked and tender.

Meanwhile, make the dressing by mixing together the ingredients in a bowl.

When the chicken is cool enough to handle, cut or tear it into strips and mix the pieces with 2 tablespoons of the dressing. Allow to cool.

Toss all the vegetables and herbs together and arrange in serving dishes. Sprinkle with the cold chicken and serve immediately with the remaining dressing.

For Asian steamed-shrimp salad with peanuts, use 1 lb medium-size raw, peeled shrimp steamed in the same way as the chicken for 2–3 minutes until pink and firm. Finish with a couple of tablespoons of crushed unsalted peanuts.

chicken with spring vegetables

Serves **4**

Preparation time **10 minutes**, plus resting

Cooking time **about 1¼ hours**

3 lb **chicken**

about 6 cups hot **chicken stock**

2 **shallots**, halved

2 **garlic cloves**

2 sprigs of **parsley**

2 sprigs of **marjoram**

2 sprigs of **lemon thyme**

2 **carrots**, halved

1 **leek**, trimmed and sliced

7 oz **tenderstem broccoli**

8 oz **asparagus**, trimmed

½ **Savoy cabbage**, shredded

Put the chicken in a large saucepan and pour over enough stock just to cover the chicken. Push the shallots, garlic, herbs, carrots, and leek into the pan and place over a medium-high heat. Bring to a boil, then reduce the heat and simmer gently for 1 hour or until the chicken is falling away from the bones.

Add the remaining vegetables to the pan and simmer for an additional 6–8 minutes or until the vegetables are cooked.

Turn off the heat and allow to rest for 5–10 minutes before serving the chicken and vegetables in deep bowls with spoonfuls of the broth. Remove the skin, if preferred, and serve with plenty of crusty bread.

For Chinese chicken soup, use the same amount of stock but omit all the vegetables and herbs. Instead, use a sliced 3 inch length of fresh ginger root, 2 garlic cloves, sliced, 1 teaspoon Chinese five spice powder, 4–5 whole star anise, and 6 tablespoons dark soy sauce. Add baby corn and snow peas instead of the spring vegetables and cook as above.

lemon chili chicken

Serves **4**

Preparation time **25 minutes**,
  plus marinating

Cooking time **45 minutes**

3½ lb **chicken**, cut into 8
  pieces

8 **garlic cloves**

4 juicy **lemons**, squeezed,
  skins reserved

1 small **red chili**, seeded and
  chopped

2 tablespoons **orange flower
  honey**

4 tablespoons chopped
  parsley, plus sprigs
  to garnish

salt and **pepper**

Arrange the chicken pieces in a shallow flameproof dish. Peel and crush 2 of the garlic cloves and add them to the lemon juice with the chili and honey. Stir well, then pour this mixture over the chicken. Tuck the lemon skins around the meat, cover and allow to marinate in the refrigerator for at least 2 hours or overnight, turning once or twice.

Turn the chicken pieces so they are skin side up, sprinkle with the remaining whole garlic cloves and put the lemon skins, cut sides down, on top.

Cook the chicken in a preheated oven, 400°F, for 45 minutes or until golden brown and tender. Stir in the parsley, season to taste, and serve garnished with parsley sprigs.

For cilantro rice & peas to serve as an accompaniment, boil 1⅔ cups frozen peas for about 3 minutes, drain them and toss them in ¼ cup melted butter with 2 chopped scallions and a handful of chopped fresh cilantro. Fork the peas into the rice and serve.

chicken with spiced rice

Serves **4**
Preparation time **5 minutes**
Cooking time **30–35 minutes**

4 boneless, skinless **chicken breasts**, about 5 oz each
4 tablespoons **olive oil**
1 **onion**, finely chopped
2 **garlic cloves**, crushed
2 teaspoons **ground cinnamon**
1 teaspoon **ground allspice**
¼ teaspoon **cayenne pepper**
1 teaspoon **salt**
¼ teaspoon **ground cloves**
½ teaspoon **ground nutmeg**
½ teaspoon **ground ginger**
½ teaspoon **black pepper**
1½ cups **long-grain rice**
3 cups hot **chicken stock**
2 tablespoons finely chopped **parsley**, to garnish

Brush the chicken breasts with 1 tablespoon of the oil and cook under a preheated hot broiler or in a griddle pan for about 1 minute on each side until golden brown but not cooked through. Set aside.

Heat the remaining oil in a large, heavy pan or casserole over a medium heat and cook the onion for 5–6 minutes or until softened. Stir in the garlic and cook for 1 minute, then add the spices and seasoning. Continue cooking, stirring frequently, for an additional 2 minutes.

Add the rice to the spice mixture, stirring well so that each grain is coated, then pour in the stock and return the chicken to the pan. Bring to a boil and cover with a tight-fitting lid, then reduce the heat and allow to simmer gently over a medium-low heat for about 15–20 minutes until the chicken and rice are cooked.

Sprinkle with parsley and serve.

For spiced-rice stuffed roast chicken, prepare the rice as above, cooking for a total of 10 minutes. Drain, reserving the stock. Use the rice to stuff a 3 lb roasting chicken. Place the chicken in a casserole dish, season, then pour the stock into the dish and add ⅔ cup white wine. Cover and roast at 375°F for 1¼ hours. Uncover, baste with the pan juices and roast for an additional 30 minutes.

chicken alla milanese

Serves **4**

Preparation time **12 minutes**

Cooking time **20 minutes**

2 lb **floury potatoes**, peeled and cut in half

4 boneless, skinless **chicken breasts**, about 5 oz each

2 small **eggs**, beaten

3 tablespoons **olive oil**

⅔ cup **butter**

4 ripe **tomatoes**, roughly chopped

2 tablespoons **capers in brine**, drained and rinsed

4 tablespoons **white wine**

4 tablespoons **lemon juice**

2 cups **arugula**

salt and **pepper**

Crust

2 teaspoons **dried oregano**

2 cups **bread crumbs**

½ teaspoon **garlic powder**

finely grated zest of 1 **lemon**

½ cup finely grated **Parmesan cheese**

Cook the potatoes in lightly salted boiling water for about 20 minutes or until soft.

Meanwhile, mix together the ingredients for the crust and tip the mixture onto a plate. Put the chicken breasts between 2 sheets of plastic wrap or waxed paper and batter with a rolling pin or mallet until flat. Dip the chicken into the beaten egg, then press into the crust mixture to coat.

Heat the oil in a large skillet and cook the chicken for 3 minutes on each side or until cooked through and golden. Set aside and keep warm.

Add half the butter to the pan and stir in the tomatoes, capers, and white wine. Season and allow to bubble for 2–3 minutes.

Drain and mash the potatoes with the lemon juice, the remaining butter, and plenty of seasoning. Spoon onto serving plates with the crispy chicken. Quickly stir the arugula into the tomatoes and pile a little onto each piece of chicken. Serve immediately.

For spinach with raisins & pine nuts to serve as an accompaniment, put 1 chopped onion, 4 tablespoons raisins, and ¼ cup butter in a large pan. Add 2 lb spinach and 3 tablespoons water. Cover and cook for 3–5 minutes, shaking the pan occasionally, until the spinach has wilted. Mix well and serve.

honey-spiced chicken breasts

Serves **4**
Preparation time **8 minutes**
Cooking time **20–25 minutes**

4 boneless **chicken breasts**,
   with skins, about 5 oz each

Spiced honey
2 tablespoons **mango
   chutney**
1 tablespoon **honey**
2 teaspoons **Worcestershire
   sauce**
1 teaspoon **garlic powder**
1 teaspoon **piri piri sauce**
2 tablespoons **red wine
   vinegar**
2 teaspoons **wholegrain
   mustard**
salt and **pepper**

Slash the chicken breasts 3–4 times with a sharp knife, then place in a baking dish.

Mix together all the ingredients for the spiced honey and spoon over the chicken. Toss until well coated.

Put the chicken in a preheated oven, 425°F, for 20–25 minutes or until the meat is cooked through and the skin is crispy.

Allow the chicken to rest for a few minutes before serving with chunky potato fries, if desired.

For herbed honey chicken with sweet potato fries, replace the spiced honey with a herbed honey sauce, as follows. Mix 2 tablespoons of honey and 2 tablespoons cider vinegar with 1 tablespoon each of chopped thyme, tarragon, and sage. Spoon over the chicken, as above, and serve with chunky sweet potato fries, if desired.

crispy duck with ginger & orange

Serves **4**

Preparation time **10 minutes**

Cooking time **24–26 minutes**

1 teaspoon **vegetable oil**

4 **duck breasts**, skin slashed

4½ cups **collard greens**,
shredded

1 tablespoon **balsamic
vinegar**

1 piece **conserved ginger in
syrup,** chopped

3 tablespoons strong **orange
and cinnamon tea** infusion
(or other citrus tea)

½ teaspoon **mixed
peppercorns**, crushed

salt

Heat the oil in a skillet over a medium heat and fry the duck breasts, skin-side down, for about 15 minutes until the skin is really crispy. Drain off the excess fat, turn the duck over and fry for an additional 5 minutes. Remove and keep warm.

Put the collard greens in a steamer over a pan of boiling water and steam for 2–3 minutes or until wilted.

Add the remaining ingredients to the skillet and season with salt to taste, then stir to mix and allow to bubble for 2–3 minutes.

Serve the duck breasts with the sauce poured over and with the steamed collard greens.

For duck with sherry-lime marmalade, omit the vinegar, ginger, and tea and instead make a sauce with 4 tablespoons dry sherry and 4 tablespoons lime marmalade. Sprinkle a handful of chopped mint onto the collard greens before serving.

thai chicken shells with cilantro

Serves **4**
Preparation time **10 minutes**
Cooking time **15 minutes**

1 teaspoon **vegetable oil**
2 **chicken breasts**, about
  5 oz each, sliced
1 tablespoon red or green
  Thai curry paste
1¾ cups **coconut milk**
1¼ cups **basmati rice**
3 tablespoons chopped
  cilantro
3 **scallions**, sliced
4 small **crisphead lettuces**,
  separated into individual
  leaves
2 **limes**, cut into wedges

Heat the oil in a nonstick skillet, add the chicken and fry for 2 minutes.

Add the curry paste and continue to fry for 1 minute, then add half the coconut milk, bring to a boil, and simmer gently for 10 minutes.

Meanwhile, put the rice in a saucepan with the remaining coconut milk and 6 tablespoons water. Bring to a boil, then reduce the heat, cover, and simmer for 10–12 minutes until the liquid is absorbed, adding a little extra water if necessary. Turn the heat off and stir in the cilantro.

Put chicken and scallion slices and some rice on a lettuce leaf and squeeze the lime wedges over the filled shells before eating.

For quick Chinese-style stir-fry, cook 10 oz chicken strips for 1 minute in 3 tablespoons vegetable oil with 1 tablespoon chopped garlic. Add 1 cup sliced green bell pepper and 5 seeded and sliced red chilies and cook for a minute, then stir in 1 small sliced onion, 1 tablespoon oyster sauce, 1 teaspoon fish sauce, ½ tablespoon light soy sauce, and ¼ teaspoon dark soy sauce. Stir-fry until the chicken is cooked through then serve.

smoked duck salad

Serves **4**

Preparation time **15 minutes**

4 cups **corn salad**

1½ **oranges** or **blood oranges**, cut into segments

4 oz **smoked duck breast**, thinly sliced

seeds of 1 **pomegranate**

½ cup **shelled pistachios**

Dressing

juice of ½ **blood orange**

1 small **shallot**, finely chopped

1 tablespoon **red wine vinegar**

1 teaspoon **wholegrain mustard**

4 tablespoons **olive oil**

Arrange the corn salad on 4 large serving plates, add the orange segments and slices of duck. Sprinkle with the pomegranate seeds and pistachios.

Make the dressing by putting the ingredients in a screw-top jar and shaking well to combine. Drizzle the dressing over each salad, and serve immediately.

For duck & watercress salad with cranberries & pecans, replace the corn salad with watercress and the pomegranate seeds and pistachios with 4 tablespoons dried cranberries and ⅓ cup chopped pecans.

baked turkey burrito

Serves **4**
Preparation time **12 minutes**
Cooking time **30–33 minutes**

4 tablespoons **vegetable oil**
1 lb **turkey breast**, thinly
  sliced
1 large **onion**, sliced
1 **red bell pepper**, cored,
  seeded, and sliced
1 **yellow bell pepper**, cored,
  seeded, and sliced
5 oz can **red kidney beans**,
  rinsed and drained
1 cup **cooked rice**
juice of **1 lime**
8 medium-size **plain flour
  tortillas**
6 tablespoons medium-hot
  ready-made **salsa**
2 tablespoons sliced,
  **preserved jalapeño
  peppers** (optional)
2 cups grated **cheddar
  cheese**
salt and **pepper**

To serve
guacamole
½ **iceberg lettuce**, shredded

Heat 2 tablespoons of the oil in a large skillet and stir-fry the sliced turkey for 3–4 minutes until it is beginning to brown, then remove it with a slotted spoon. Increase the heat, add the remaining oil, and fry the onion and bell peppers for 5–6 minutes, stirring only occasionally so that they brown quickly without softening too much.

Reduce the heat, return the turkey to the pan and stir in the beans and cooked rice. Season well, squeeze over the lime juice and remove from the heat. Spoon the filling onto the tortillas, roll them up and arrange them in a rectangular ovenproof dish.

Pour the salsa over the tortillas and sprinkle with the jalapeño peppers (if used) and cheddar. Cook in a preheated oven, 400°F, for about 20 minutes, until hot and the cheese has melted. Serve immediately with guacamole and shredded lettuce.

For hot tomato salsa to serve as an accompaniment, chop 1 lb tomatoes, 1 hot red chili, 1 garlic clove, and 1 small onion. Add 2 tablespoons tomato paste, 2 tablespoons red wine vinegar, and 2 tablespoons sugar. Mix well. Alternatively, blend all the ingredients in a food processor until finely chopped.

roast poussins with oregano

Serves **4**

Preparation time **10 minutes**, plus resting

Cooking time **55 minutes**

¼ cup **butter**

finely grated zest of **1 lemon**

2 tablespoons **oregano**, chopped

1 large **garlic clove**, crushed

2 **poussins**, about 1 lb each

4 cups **peppery mixed salad leaves**

salt and **pepper**

Mash together the butter, lemon zest, oregano, garlic, and seasoning. Lift the skin from the poussins and slide the flavored butter between the flesh and skin, or, if you prefer, smear the butter over the skin.

Put the poussins side by side in a roasting pan and cook in a preheated oven, 425°F, for about 55 minutes, basting occasionally, until golden and crispy and the juices run clear. Remove from the oven and allow to rest for 5 minutes.

Transfer the poussins to a cutting board and use a long, sharp knife to cut each one carefully in half lengthwise. Serve immediately with the salad leaves.

For classic potato gratin, to serve as an accompaniment and which can be cooked in the oven at the same time as the poussins, use 1½ lb peeled and thinly sliced potatoes, blanched for a minute or two in boiling, salted water. Drain the potatoes and tip them into a large, ovenproof dish. Sprinkle with 2 finely chopped garlic cloves and season. Pour over 1½ cups heavy cream and sprinkle with a little grated nutmeg. Dot with ¼ cup butter, then put the dish in the oven for around 45 minutes or until soft when pierced with a knife.

hot duck & coconut noodles

Serves **4**
Preparation time **10 minutes**
Cooking time **15 minutes**

4 **confit duck legs**
1 cup **coconut milk**
¾ cup **chicken stock**
2 tablespoons **Thai fish sauce**
3 whole **star anise**
1 teaspoon **dried red pepper flakes**
1 inch piece **fresh ginger root**, thinly sliced
1 small bunch of **cilantro**, chopped
juice of 2 **limes**
8 oz **flat rice noodles**
4 tablespoons **coconut shavings**, toasted
⅓ cup **cashew nuts**, toasted

Heat a large skillet and put the duck legs and their fat, skin-side down, in the pan. Cook over a medium heat for 10 minutes until the skins turn golden and crispy. Turn and cook for an additional 2–3 minutes until the legs are heated through. Drain on paper towels, then tear the meat into small pieces and discard the bones.

Meanwhile, pour the coconut milk into a pan with the stock, fish sauce, star anise, pepper flakes, ginger, and half the chopped cilantro and bring to simmering point. Allow to bubble gently for 10 minutes to let the flavors infuse. Stir in the lime juice.

Cook the noodles in unsalted boiling water for about 3 minutes or according to the instructions on the package, then drain and heap into serving bowls.

Top with the duck meat and pour over the hot coconut broth. Sprinkle with the coconut shavings, cashews, and remaining cilantro. Serve immediately.

For spiced shrimp stir-fry, omit the duck and instead mix 13 oz raw shrimp with a 1 inch piece of fresh ginger, grated, 1 crushed garlic clove, 1 freshly chopped red chili and 1 tablespoon vegetable oil. Heat a wok until smoking, add another tablespoon vegetable oil and stir-fry the shrimp for 2–3 minutes until pink and cooked through. Serve with the noodles and a ladle of the hot coconut broth, finishing as before with cashews and cilantro.

chicken with spinach chermoula

Serves **4**
Preparation time **12 minutes**
Cooking time **25 minutes**

4 boneless, skinless **chicken breasts**, about 6 oz each, cut into large pieces
2 tablespoons **olive oil**
1 large **red onion**, sliced
13 oz can **chickpeas**, rinsed and drained
8 ready-to-eat **dried apricots**, sliced
pinch of **saffron**
4 cups **spinach leaves**, stalks removed
½ small **preserved lemon**, finely diced (optional)
small bunch of **cilantro**, roughly chopped
small bunch of **flat leaf parsley**, roughly chopped

Chermoula
3 tablespoons ready-made **chermoula mix**
1 teaspoon **harissa paste**
juice of 1 **lemon**
6 tablespoons **olive oil**

Make the chermoula by putting all the ingredients in a screw-top jar and shaking to combine. Mix half the paste with the chicken and set aside.

Heat the oil in a large skillet over a medium heat and fry the onion for about 8 minutes until soft and golden. Increase the heat a little, tip in the coated chicken and cook for about 12 minutes, stirring frequently. Stir in the chickpeas, apricots, saffron, and the remaining chermoula paste and cook for an additional 3–4 minutes. The chicken and spices should be cooked through.

Stir in the spinach and cook until just wilted, then add the preserved lemon (if used) and herbs. Serve immediately on warm pita or flat breads.

For homemade chermoula, instead of the ready-made chermoula mix, stir together 2 teaspoons ground cumin, 2 teaspoons ground coriander, 1 teaspoon turmeric, 1 teaspoon salt, and 1 teaspoon ground black pepper.

turkey & pumpkin seed salad

Serves **4**
Preparation time **12 minutes**
Cooking time **6 minutes**

3 tablespoons **sunflower oil**
13 oz ground **turkey**
1 tablespoon **preserved**
  jalapeño peppers, sliced
7 oz can **corn**, drained
1 ripe **avocado**, peeled, pitted,
  and cut into chunks
2 ripe **tomatoes**, chopped
1 small **red onion**, finely diced
small bunch of **cilantro,**
  chopped
salt and **pepper**

Dressing
juice of **2 limes**
1 teaspoon **honey**
4 tablespoons **pumpkin**
  seed oil

To serve
½ small **red cabbage,**
  shredded
8 oz **buffalo mozzarella**
  cheese, cubed
4 **taco shells**
3 tablespoons **pumpkin**
  seeds, to sprinkle

Make the dressing by mixing together the ingredients in a small bowl. Season to taste and set aside.

Heat the oil in a large skillet and fry the turkey for 5–6 minutes until cooked and beginning to brown. Scrape into a bowl, mix with half the dressing and set aside to cool.

Make a chunky salsa by combining the peppers, corn, avocado, tomatoes, red onion, and cilantro. Mix with the remaining dressing.

When the turkey is cool, mix it with the salsa and serve with the cabbage, mozzarella, and taco shells, sprinkled with the pumpkin seeds.

For turkey with white cabbage & sunflower seed salad, replace the pumpkin seed oil in the dressing with olive oil and the red cabbage with white cabbage. Substitute the mozzarella with finely diced Gruyére or Gouda and the pumpkin seeds with sunflower seeds. Omit the tacos, serving the salad as a base with the turkey mix on top.

turkey & wild mushroom pasties

Serves **4**

Preparation time **8 minutes**,
  plus soaking

Cooking time **29–32 minutes**

⅔ cup **dried wild mushrooms**

4 tablespoons **olive oil**

1 lb **turkey breast**, sliced

3 oz **prosciutto**, torn into
  pieces

3 cups trimmed and sliced
  field or **portabello**
  mushrooms

6 tablespoons **red wine**

1 teaspoon chopped **thyme**

8 oz **mascarpone cheese**

1 lb **puff pastry** (thawed if
  frozen)

1 **egg**, beaten

salt and **pepper**

watercress, to garnish

Soak the mushrooms in 4 tablespoons boiling water for 5–10 minutes. Heat 2 tablespoons of the oil in a skillet and fry the turkey for 2–3 minutes until golden. Add the prosciutto and cook for 2 minutes before adding the fresh and dried mushrooms. Fry for 3–4 minutes until the mushrooms are soft and golden.

Pour the wine into the pan, then add the thyme. Allow the liquid to bubble for 2–3 minutes until evaporated. Remove from the heat, stir in the mascarpone, and season to taste.

Roll out the pastry into a rectangular shape until it forms a thin layer and cut into four. Spoon one-quarter of the mixture onto the center of each quarter of pastry. Brush a little beaten egg around the edges, fold over the pastry, and press firmly to seal.

Brush the remaining egg over the closed pasties, score the tops with a knife, if desired, and cook in a preheated oven, 400°F, for 20 minutes until golden and crispy.

For turkey & mushroom pie, increase the wine to 1¼ cups and simmer for 5 minutes. Finish the filling as above. Replace the puff pastry with shortcrust. Roll it out into a thick layer to cover a 9 inch pie dish with an overlap of 2 inches. Cut a strip of pastry ½ inch wide and put it round the rim of the dish. Add the filling and cover with the remaining pastry. Glaze with egg and bake in a preheated oven, 400°F, for 20 minutes then lower the heat to 350°F, for an additional 10–15 minutes.

spicy basque-style chicken

Serves **4**
Preparation time **12 minutes**
Cooking time **45–47 minutes**

2 lb **chicken pieces** (thighs,
   drumsticks, etc.)
1 heaping tablespoon
   seasoned flour
3 tablespoons **olive oil**
1 **onion**, sliced
1 **red bell pepper**, cored,
   seeded, and sliced
1 **green bell pepper**, cored,
   seeded, and sliced
2 **garlic cloves**, crushed
1 teaspoon **paprika**
1 teaspoon **hot smoked**
   paprika
3 oz **prosciutto**, torn into
   pieces
5 tablespoons **Marsala**
⅔ cup **white wine**
13 oz can **chopped tomatoes**
1 teaspoon **dried thyme**
salt and **pepper**

Dust the chicken in the seasoned flour. Heat the oil in a large, heavy casserole over a medium-high heat and fry the chicken until golden brown. Remove and set aside.

Reduce the heat, add the onion and peppers and cook, stirring frequently, for 4–5 minutes until softened and golden. Stir in the garlic, paprikas, and prosciutto and fry for an additional 1–2 minutes.

Return the chicken to the pan, pour in the Marsala, wine, 6 tablespoons water, and the tomatoes. Stir in the thyme and season to taste. Bring to a boil, then reduce the heat to a simmer, cover the pan and leave for 30–35 minutes until the chicken is cooked and the sauce is rich and thick.

Serve the chicken in bowls with lots of sauce.

For pan-fried polenta with olives to serve as an accompaniment, cut 2 x 1 lb packages of ready-made polenta into 1 inch slices. Fry the slices in olive oil and sprinkle with 2 tablespoons chopped black olives and 1 teaspoon chopped fresh parsley. Add 1 crushed garlic clove and fry quickly. Serve as above.

fish

pan-fried haddock fillets

Serves **4**

Preparation time **15 minutes**

Cooking time **20 minutes**

2 lb **floury potatoes**, peeled

5 tablespoons **whole milk**

⅔ cup **butter**

4 **haddock fillets**, about
  5 oz each, skin on

2 tablespoons **capers in
  brine**, drained and rinsed

4 tablespoons **lemon juice**

salt and **pepper**

Cook the potatoes in lightly salted boiling water for about 20 minutes. Mash until smooth with the milk and ¼ cup of the butter. Season well.

Meanwhile, melt the remaining butter in a large skillet, add the haddock fillets, skin-side down, and cook for about 3 minutes until golden and crispy. Carefully turn over the fillets and cook for an additional 1–2 minutes.

Remove the fillets and transfer to serving plates with the mashed potato.

Return the pan to the burner. Increase the heat until the butter turns nut-brown in color, then add the capers and lemon juice. Bubble for a minute and then spoon over the fish and potatoes. Serve immediately.

For trout fillets with almonds, replace the haddock fillets with trout fillets and fry as above, finishing with almonds instead of capers.

jumbo shrimp with japanese salad

Serves **4**

Preparation time **10 minutes, plus cooling**

Cooking time **3 minutes**

13 oz **raw, peeled jumbo shrimp**

3 cups **bean sprouts**

4 oz **snow peas**, shredded

½ cup thinly sliced **water chestnuts**

½ **iceberg lettuce**, shredded

12 **radishes**, thinly sliced

1 tablespoon **sesame seeds**, lightly toasted

Dressing

2 tablespoons **rice vinegar**

½ cup **sunflower oil**

1 teaspoon **five spice powder** (optional)

2 tablespoons **mirin**

Set a steamer over a pan of simmering water and steam the jumbo shrimp for 2–3 minutes until cooked and pink. Set aside and allow to cool.

Make the dressing by mixing together all the ingredients in a small bowl.

Toss together the bean sprouts, snow peas, water chestnuts, lettuce, and radishes and sprinkle with the shrimp and sesame seeds. Drizzle over the dressing and serve immediately.

For chili sauce to serve as an accompaniment, combine 1 finely chopped garlic clove, ½ teaspoon finely grated fresh ginger root, 2 teaspoons light soy sauce, 1 tablespoon sweet chili sauce, and ½ tablespoon tomato ketchup. Mix well.

lima bean & anchovy pâté

Serves **2–3**
Preparation time **5 minutes**

14 oz can **lima beans**,
   drained and rinsed
2 oz can **anchovy fillets** in oil
2 **scallions**, finely chopped
2 tablespoons **lemon juice**
1 tablespoon **olive oil**
4 tablespoons chopped
   cilantro
salt and **pepper**

To serve
lemon wedges
4–6 slices **rye bread**, toasted

Put all the ingredients except the cilantro in a food processor or blender and process until well mixed but not smooth. Alternatively, mash the beans with a fork, finely chop the anchovies, and mix the ingredients together by hand.

Stir in the cilantro and season well. Serve with lemon wedges and accompanied with toasted rye bread.

For lima bean & mushroom pâté, replace the anchovies with 3 cups sliced mushrooms. Cook these in 2 tablespoons olive oil with 1 finely chopped garlic clove until greatly reduced and all juices have evaporated. Cool. Puree the mushrooms in a food processor or blender, or mash with a fork, and add the lima beans, processing or mixing as above.

quick tuna steak with green salsa

Serves **4**
Preparation time **14 minutes**,
   plus marinating
Cooking time **2–4 minutes**

2 tablespoons **olive oil**
grated zest of 1 **lemon**
2 teaspoons chopped **parsley**
½ teaspoon crushed **coriander
   seeds**
4 fresh **tuna steaks**, about
   5 oz each
salt and **pepper**
dressed **lettuce salad**,
   to serve

Salsa
2 tablespoons **capers**,
   chopped
2 tablespoons chopped
   cornichons
1 tablespoon finely chopped
   parsley
2 teaspoons chopped **chives**
2 teaspoons finely chopped
   chervil
¼ cup pitted **green olives**,
   chopped
1 **shallot**, finely chopped
   (optional)
2 tablespoons **lemon juice**
2 tablespoons **olive oil**

Mix together the oil, lemon zest, parsley, and coriander seeds with plenty of pepper in a bowl. Rub the tuna steaks with the mixture.

Combine the ingredients for the salsa, season to taste, and set aside.

Heat a griddle or skillet until hot and cook the tuna steaks for 1–2 minutes on each side to cook partially. The tuna should be well seared but rare. Remove and allow to rest for a couple of minutes.

Serve the tuna steaks with a spoonful of salsa, a dressed salad, and plenty of fresh crusty bread.

For yellow pepper & mustard salsa, combine the following: 2 yellow bell peppers, finely chopped; 1 tablespoon Dijon mustard; 2 tablespoons each finely chopped chives, parsley, and dill; 1 teaspoon sugar; 1 tablespoon cider vinegar, and 2 tablespoons olive oil.

scallops with pancetta

Serves **4**

Preparation time **10 minutes**, plus cooling time

Cooking time **15 minutes**

8 small vine-ripened **tomatoes**, halved

2 **garlic cloves**, finely chopped

8 **basil leaves**

2 tablespoons **olive oil**

2 tablespoons **balsamic vinegar**

8 thin slices of **pancetta**

16–20 **sea scallops**, corals and muscles removed

8 canned **artichoke hearts in oil**, drained and halved

3 cups **corn salad**, trimmed

salt and **pepper**

Arrange the tomatoes close together, cut side up, in a roasting pan. Sprinkle with the chopped garlic and basil, drizzle with 1 tablespoon each of the oil and balsamic vinegar, and season well with salt and pepper. Cook in a preheated oven, 425°F, for 15 minutes.

Meanwhile, cook the pancetta slices in a preheated hot griddle pan for about 2 minutes, turning once, until crisp and golden. Transfer to a plate lined with paper towels until needed.

Quickly sear the scallops for 1 minute in the hot griddle, then turn them over and cook for an additional minute on the other side until cooked and starting to caramelize. Remove, cover with foil, and allow to rest for 2 minutes.

Meanwhile, cook the artichoke hearts for about 2 minutes until hot and charred.

Toss the corn salad with the remaining oil and balsamic vinegar and arrange on serving plates. Top with the artichokes, tomatoes, crispy pancetta, and scallops. Serve immediately.

For salmon & pancetta salad, omit the tomatoes and cook the pancetta, as above. Instead of the scallops, use a chunky 1 lb fresh salmon fillet. Brush the salmon lightly with olive oil before searing on a hot griddle for 2–3 minutes until golden, turning once. Cook the artichoke hearts as above. Substitute the corn salad with arugula and shredded crisphead lettuce hearts. Toss and arrange as above.

shrimp with sesame noodles

Serves **4**
Preparation time **8 minutes**
Cooking time **6 minutes**

8 oz **egg noodles**
1 tablespoon **sesame oil**, plus
  extra to serve
1 tablespoon **vegetable oil**
1 **yellow bell pepper**, cored,
  seeded, and sliced
1 **red bell pepper**, cored,
  seeded, and sliced
3 oz **shiitake** or **chestnut**
  mushrooms, trimmed and
  thinly sliced
1 large **carrot**, peeled and cut
  into thin sticks
2 **scallions**, thinly sliced
  lengthwise
1 **red chili**, finely chopped
10 oz **large cooked peeled**
  shrimp
1 tablespoon **sesame seeds**,
  lightly toasted

Cook the noodles in a large saucepan of unsalted water for 4 minutes or according to the instructions on the package.

Meanwhile, heat a large wok over a high heat until smoking. Add the oils and stir-fry the peppers for 1–2 minutes. Add the mushrooms, cook for 1 minute, then add the carrot and cook for an additional minute. Add the scallions, chili, and shrimp and stir-fry for 2 minutes.

Drain the noodles and add them to the wok. Mix to combine, heat through, then sprinkle with the sesame seeds and serve immediately.

For teriyaki shrimp with vegetables on soba, substitute the egg noodles with soba noodles (made with buckwheat flour). Prepare the vegetables and noodles as above but cook the shrimp separately, adding 1 sliced garlic clove and 4 tablespoons ready-made teriyaki sauce. Serve the shrimp on the soba noodles and sprinkle with cilantro instead of sesame seeds.

crunchy swordfish with puy lentils

Serves **4**

Preparation time **12 minutes**

Cooking time **15 minutes**

4 skinless **swordfish fillets**,
about 6 oz each

2 tablespoons **olive oil**

5 cups cooked **Puy lentils**,
heated

8 **sun-blushed tomatoes**,
roughly chopped

small bunch of **basil**, shredded

1 tablespoon **capers in brine**,
drained and rinsed

4 **scallions**, finely sliced

8 pitted **black olives**, roughly
chopped

2 tablespoons **olive oil**

salt and **pepper**

2 **lemons**, halved, to serve

Crust

1½ cups **bread crumbs**

grated zest of 1 **lemon**

1 teaspoon finely chopped
rosemary

2 tablespoons finely chopped
parsley

Mix together the ingredients for the crust and add
some salt and pepper. Rub the fish fillets in the oil
and then press them into the crust mixture to coat.

Transfer the fish to a nonstick baking sheet and
carefully tip over the remaining crust. Cook in a
preheated oven, 425°F, for 15 minutes until the
fish is flaky and the crust is golden and crunchy.

Put the hot lentils in a bowl and stir in the remaining
ingredients. Serve immediately with the fish fillets and
lemon halves.

For crunchy hake with Mediterranean potatoes,
replace the swordfish with 4 x 7 oz hake steaks and
prepare as above. Instead of the lentils, peel and halve
1½ lb red new potatoes, boil them for 10–15 minutes,
drain, then toss with the other ingredients.

blackened cod with citrus salsa

Serves **4**
Preparation time **15 minutes**
Cooking time **15 minutes**

1 large **orange**
1 **garlic clove**, crushed
2 large **tomatoes**, seeded
  and diced
2 tablespoons chopped **basil**,
  plus extra to garnish
½ cup pitted **black olives**,
  chopped
5 tablespoons **olive oil**
4 **cod fillets**, about 6 oz each
1 tablespoon **jerk seasoning**
salt and **pepper**

Cut the skin and the white membrane off the orange. Working over a bowl to catch the juice, cut between the membranes to remove the segments. Halve the segments and mix them with the reserved juice and the garlic, tomatoes, basil, olives, and 4 tablespoons of the oil. Season to taste with salt and pepper and set aside to infuse.

Brush the cod with the remaining oil and coat with the jerk seasoning. Heat a large, heavy skillet and cook the cod, skin-side down, for 5 minutes. Turn the fish over and cook for an additional 3 minutes. Transfer to a preheated oven, 300°F, to rest for about 5 minutes. Garnish the fish with basil and serve with the salsa and a green salad.

For quick crumbed cod, mix together 3 tablespoons each bread crumbs, torn basil leaves, and grated Parmesan cheese, 2 pieces drained and chopped sun-dried tomato, 1 tablespoon olive oil, and the grated zest of 1 lemon. Press the mixture over 4 pieces of cod, each 6 oz, and cook in a preheated oven, 375°F, for 20 minutes.

salmon fillets with sage & quinoa

Serves **4**
Preparation time **5 minutes**
Cooking time **15 minutes**

1 cup **quinoa**
½ cup **butter**, at room
   temperature
8 **sage leaves**, chopped
small bunch of **chives**
grated zest and juice of
   1 lemon
4 **salmon fillet steaks**, about
   4 oz each
1 tablespoon **olive oil**
salt and **pepper**

Cook the quinoa in unsalted boiling water for about
15 minutes or until cooked but firm.

Meanwhile, mix the butter with the sage, chives, and
lemon zest and add salt and pepper to taste.

Rub the salmon steaks with the oil, season with pepper
and cook in a preheated hot griddle pan for about
6 minutes, turning carefully once. Remove and set
aside to rest.

Drain the quinoa, stir in the lemon juice and season
to taste. Spoon onto serving plates and top with the
salmon, topping each piece with a knob of sage butter.

For salmon with tarragon & couscous, replace
the sage leaves with 4 sprigs of tarragon and the
quinoa with 1½ cups couscous. Soak the couscous
in 1¾ cups just-boiled water for 5–8 minutes until the
grains are soft. Fluff the couscous with a fork and
season. Dress with a little lemon juice and olive oil
and serve with the salmon, as above.

cod fillet with tomatoes & arugula

Serves **4**
Preparation time **5 minutes**
Cooking time **12–15 minutes**

4 chunky **cod fillets**, about
   5 oz each
3 tablespoons **olive oil**
2 **garlic cloves**, chopped
10 oz **cherry tomatoes on
   the vine**
2 tablespoons **balsamic
   vinegar**
4 tablespoons shredded **basil**
2½ cups **arugula leaves**
salt and **pepper**

Rub the cod fillets all over with 1 tablespoon of the oil and season well. Sprinkle with the garlic and put the fish in a baking tray. Arrange the cherry tomatoes alongside and drizzle with the remaining oil, the balsamic vinegar, and basil. Season to taste.

Transfer the tray to a preheated oven, 425°F, and cook for 12–15 minutes until the fish is flaky and the tomatoes roasted.

Serve the cod with the tomatoes and arugula leaves.

For cod with Italian-style salsa, fry the cod fillets for 5–6 minutes until cooked and golden brown. To make the salsa, combine 8 finely chopped sun-dried tomatoes, 2 tablespoons roughly chopped basil leaves, 1 tablespoon drained capers, 1 tablespoon lightly crushed toasted pine nuts, and 2 tablespoons olive oil. Serve with an arugula salad.

mussel & lemon curry

Serves **4**

Preparation time **15 minutes**

Cooking time **15 minutes**

2 lb **mussels**, scrubbed and debearded

½ cup **lager**

½ cup **unsalted butter**

1 **onion**, chopped

1 **garlic clove**, crushed

1 inch **fresh ginger root**, peeled and grated

1 tablespoon medium **curry powder**

⅔ cup **light cream**

2 tablespoons **lemon juice**

salt and **pepper**

chopped **parsley**, to garnish

Discard any mussels that are broken or do not close immediately when sharply tapped with a knife. Put them in a large saucepan with the lager, cover, and cook, shaking the pan frequently, for 4 minutes until all the shells have opened. Discard any that remain closed. Strain, reserve the cooking liquid and keep it warm.

Meanwhile, melt the butter in a large saucepan and fry the onion, garlic, ginger, and curry powder, stirring frequently, for 5 minutes. Strain in the reserved mussel liquid and bring to a boil. Boil until reduced by half, beat in the cream and lemon juice and simmer gently.

Stir in the mussels, warm through, and season to taste. Garnish with chopped parsley and serve with crusty bread, if desired.

For shrimp & lemon curry with warm lemon naan,

substitute the mussels with shelled raw shrimp. You will need about 10 shrimp per person, cut almost in half down the center to allow the flavors to penetrate the flesh. Cook in the same way as the mussels for 3–4 minutes until the flesh turns pink. Serve with 4 warm naan breads brushed with lemon butter, made by mixing the zest of 1 lemon with ¼ cup melted butter.

bream with new potatoes

Serves **4**
Preparation time **5 minutes**
Cooking time **20 minutes**

1 lb baby **new potatoes**
3–4 tablespoons **olive oil**
6 tablespoons fresh
  mayonnaise
1 tablespoon chopped **chervil**
½ **garlic clove**, crushed
4 boned **sea bream fillets**
2 tablespoons **lemon juice**
sea salt and **pepper**

Put the new potatoes in a large saucepan with
1–2 tablespoons of the oil. Place over a medium-low
heat and cover with a tight-fitting lid. Cook for about
20 minutes, shaking the pan frequently to move the
potatoes around. When done, the potatoes should be
cooked and crispy golden. Remove from the pan and
sprinkle with sea salt.

Meanwhile, mix together the mayonnaise with the
chervil and garlic.

Heat the remaining oil in a large skillet over a medium-
high heat. Season the fish with salt and pepper and
cook, flesh-side down, for 1 minute before turning
carefully and frying for an additional 2–3 minutes until
the skin is crispy. Squeeze over the lemon juice and
serve immediately with the crispy potatoes and garlicky
mayonnaise.

For mackerel with horseradish sour cream, replace
the chervil and garlic with 2 tablespoons horseradish
sauce and the mayonnaise with thick sour cream.
Substitute the bream with 4 mackerel fillets, seasoned
with salt and pepper and a pinch of chili powder.
Cook in the same way as the bream and serve with
new potatoes, as above.

buttery lobster tails with aïoli

Serves **4**
Preparation time **20 minutes**
Cooking time **7–8 minutes**

4 raw **lobster tails**
¼ cup **butter**
2 tablespoons **garlic-infused oil**
finely grated zest of **1 lemon**
2 tablespoons chopped **chervil**, plus extra sprigs to garnish
cucumber ribbons, to serve

Aïoli
1 large **egg yolk**
3–4 **garlic cloves**, crushed
1 tablespoon **lemon juice**
¾ cup **olive oil**
1 tablespoon snipped **chives**
salt and **pepper**

Make the aïoli. With all the ingredients at room temperature, beat the egg yolk in a bowl with the garlic, lemon juice, and a large pinch of salt and pepper, either by hand or with an electric beater. Gradually add the oil, drop by drop, beating constantly until it is all completely incorporated and you have a thick, smooth emulsion. Stir in the chives.

Dot the lobster tails with the butter and drizzle with the garlic oil. Cook the lobster tails, flesh-side up, under a preheated broiler for 7–8 minutes until cooked through. Sprinkle with the lemon zest and chopped chervil and serve immediately with cucumber ribbons and the aïoli in small bowls.

For lobster tails with sun-dried tomato sauce,
combine 2 tablespoons each of sun-dried tomato paste, mascarpone, and pesto with 2 teaspoons finely grated lemon zest and 2 teaspoons lemon juice. Season well.

coconut & cilantro mussels

Serves **4**
Preparation time **10 minutes**
Cooking time **15 minutes**

1 tablespoon **vegetable oil**
4 **scallions**, finely chopped
1 inch length **galangal** or
   fresh ginger root, shredded
1 **green chili**, finely chopped
¾ cup **coconut milk**
large bunch of **cilantro**,
   chopped, plus extra
   to garnish
1 tablespoon chopped **Thai
   basil** (optional)
¾ cup **fish stock**
2 tablespoons **Thai fish
   sauce**
2 tablespoons **lime juice**
1 tablespoon **soy sauce**
1 tablespoon **brown sugar**
3–4 **lime leaves**, shredded
   (optional)
2 lb **mussels**, scrubbed and
   debearded
shredded coconut, toasted,
   to garnish (optional)

Heat the oil in a large saucepan and cook the scallions, galangal or ginger, and chili for 2 minutes until soft. Add the remaining ingredients except the mussels and warm gently until the sugar has dissolved. Turn up the heat and bring up to boiling point, then reduce the heat and simmer gently for 5 minutes to allow the flavors to develop.

Tip the mussels into the coconut sauce and cover with a tight-fitting lid. Cook for 3–4 minutes or until the mussels have opened—discard any that have not.

Spoon into serving bowls with plenty of the juices and sprinkle with extra cilantro leaves and shredded coconut, if using. Serve immediately with steamed jasmine rice or butternut squash.

For coconut & cilantro seafood with lime rice,
replace the mussels with 1 lb fresh or frozen prepared seafood mix and cook as above, but omitting the lime leaves. Cook 1¼ cups rice with the grated zest of 1 lime. Serve the rice in bowls and ladle over the seafood. Serve with prawn crackers.

scallops with citrus dressing

Serves **4**
Preparation time **10 minutes**
Cooking time **7–9 minutes**

16 large **raw shrimp**, heads
   removed
24 fresh **scallops**, roe
   removed
1 large ripe but firm **mango**,
   peeled, pitted, and cut into
   chunks
3 cups mixed **salad leaves**

Citrus dressing
juice of ½ **pink grapefruit**
finely grated zest and juice of
   1 **lime**
1 teaspoon **honey**
1 tablespoon **raspberry
   vinegar**
5 tablespoons **lemon oil**

Make the citrus dressing by mixing together all the ingredients in a small bowl.

Poach the shrimp in simmering water for 2 minutes and drain.

Put the scallops, mango, and shrimp in a bowl and pour over 3 tablespoons of the dressing. Mix well to coat before threading them alternately on skewers.

Heat the oil in a large skillet over a medium heat and fry the skewers for about 5–7 minutes, turning and basting occasionally until golden brown and cooked.

Arrange the skewers on plates with salad leaves and serve with the remaining dressing.

For haloumi & mango kebabs with citrus dressing, replace the scallops and shrimp with 14 oz–1 lb haloumi, cut into cubes. Coat with the dressing, skewer with the mango, and fry, as above. Alternatively, cook on a barbecue for the same amount of time until slightly charred.

fried miso cod with bok choy

Serves **4**
Preparation time **10 minutes**,
  plus marinating
Cooking time **13–15 minutes**

4 **cod fillets**, about 6 oz each
olive oil, for brushing
4 heads **bok choy**, halved
  lengthwise and blanched
  in boiling water for
  1–2 minutes

Miso sauce
½ cup **miso paste**
3 tablespoons **soy sauce**
3 tablespoons **sake**
3 tablespoons **mirin**
¼ cup **superfine sugar**

Make the miso sauce. Put the miso paste, soy sauce, sake, mirin, and sugar into a small saucepan and heat gently until the sugar has dissolved. Simmer gently for about 5 minutes, stirring frequently. Remove from the heat and set aside to cool.

Arrange the cod fillets in a dish into which they fit snugly and cover with the cold miso sauce. Rub the sauce over the fillets so that they are completely covered and allow to marinate for at least 6 hours, preferably overnight.

Heat a skillet over a medium heat, remove the cod fillets from the miso sauce and cook the fish for about 2–3 minutes. Carefully turn them over and cook for an additional 2–3 minutes. Remove and keep warm.

Heat a clean pan. Brush a little oil over the cut side of the bok choy and arrange them, cut-side down, in the pan. Cook for about 2 minutes until hot and lightly charred. Transfer to a serving plate with the cod and serve immediately.

For sesame baby vegetables as an alternative accompaniment, stir-fry 7 oz baby corn for 5 minutes then add 4 oz snow peas and cook for an additional 3 minutes. Add 1 sliced zucchini and cook for another 3 minutes (total cooking time 11 minutes). Finally, toss the vegetables in 1 tablespoon light soy sauce and 1 teaspoon sesame oil and serve.

teriyaki salmon with noodles

Serves **4**
Preparation time **12 minutes**
Cooking time **15 minutes**

4 boneless, skinless **salmon
  fillets**, about 5 oz each
2 teaspoons **sesame oil**
4 **scallions**, thinly sliced
1½ cups hot **vegetable stock**
2 tablespoons **light soy
  sauce**
¼ cup **miso paste**
1 tablespoon **mirin** or
  1 teaspoon **brown sugar**
10 oz ready-cooked **udon
  noodles**
4 baby heads **bok choy**,
  halved lengthwise

Teriyaki sauce
3 tablespoons **sake**
1 teaspoon **dark soy sauce**
3 tablespoons **light soy
  sauce**
2 tablespoons **superfine
  sugar**
1 tablespoon **honey**
2 tablespoons **mirin** or extra
  sugar

Make the teriyaki sauce. Put all the ingredients in a
small saucepan and stir over a medium heat until the
sugar has dissolved. Increase the heat a little and
simmer for 5 minutes until thickened. Set aside to cool.

Rub the cooled teriyaki sauce over the salmon fillets
and arrange them in an ovenproof dish. Cook under a
preheated broiler for 4–5 minutes on each side,
basting occasionally. Remove and set aside.

Heat the sesame oil in a skillet and stir-fry the
scallions for 2 minutes. Add the stock, soy sauce, miso
paste, and mirin or sugar, stirring to dissolve. Simmer
gently and add the noodles and bok choy and cook for
2 minutes until the leaves have wilted.

Serve immediately topped with the broiled salmon.

For herb-crusted salmon with asparagus, cook
8 oz trimmed asparagus spears in boiling water for
5 minutes. Brush one side of each salmon fillet with
olive oil. Chop a small bunch of parsley and use to
coat the salmon, then griddle or fry in olive oil for
about 3 minutes on each side. Serve the salmon
topped with the asparagus spears and with some
crusty bread.

herby chickpea crab cakes

Serves **4**
Preparation time **10 minutes**
Cooking time **7 minutes**

13 oz can **chickpeas**, rinsed
  and drained
2 **scallions**, thinly sliced
3 tablespoons chopped
  parsley
2 tablespoons chopped
  chives
1 **egg yolk**
1 teaspoon **piri piri sauce**
1 teaspoon **Worcestershire**
  sauce
2 tablespoons **mayonnaise**
1⅓ cups coarse dry **bread**
  crumbs
10 oz **white crabmeat**
2 tablespoons **olive oil**

To serve
2½ cups **arugula leaves**
4 tablespoons **Aïoli** (see
  page 116)

Put the chickpeas, scallions, herbs, egg yolk, piri piri
sauce, Worcestershire sauce, mayonnaise, and ½ cup
of the bread crumbs in a food processor and process
briefly. Add the crabmeat and pulse quickly to combine,
adding more bread crumbs if the mixture is too wet.

Transfer the mixture to a bowl and form it into 4 large
or 8 small patties. Press them into the remaining bread
crumbs until well coated.

Heat the oil in a large skillet and fry the crab cakes for
about 5 minutes, turning carefully once, until crisp and
golden. Drain on paper towels and serve immediately
with arugula leaves and a dollop of aïoli.

For avocado & watercress sauce to serve instead
of the aïoli, chop 1 tablespoon capers and 2½ cups
watercress and mash 1 avocado. Mix together with
¾ cup Greek or whole milk yogurt.

squid with lemon mayonnaise

Serves **4**
Preparation time **30 minutes**
Cooking time **9 minutes**

1 lb prepared **squid**
½ cup **all-purpose flour**
1 tablespoon **paprika**
pinch of **cayenne pepper**
olive oil, for deep-frying
salt and **pepper**

Lemon and herb mayonnaise
2 **egg yolks**
½ teaspoon **wholegrain mustard**
1 tablespoon **lemon juice**, plus extra to taste
¾ cup **light olive oil**
1 tablespoon chopped **flat leaf parsley**, plus extra to garnish
1 tablespoon chopped **chervil**
1 tablespoon chopped **chives**
2 tablespoons chopped **watercress**
finely grated zest of **1 lemon**
1 small **garlic clove**, crushed
lemon wedges, to serve

Make the mayonnaise. Beat the egg yolks in a bowl with the mustard and lemon juice. Add the oil, drop by drop, beating constantly until it is incorporated and you have a thick, smooth emulsion. Season and stir in the herbs, watercress, lemon zest, and garlic, adding extra lemon juice to taste. Cover and chill until required.

Wash the squid and pat dry with paper towels. Cut the bodies into rings about ¾ inch thick. Mix together the flour, paprika, and cayenne and season well. Put the flour in a plastic bag, add the squid rings and tentacles and shake until they are coated.

Heat the oil in a large skillet or deep-fat fryer 350°F or until a cube of bread browns in 20 seconds. Remove about one-third of the squid from the bag and shake off the excess flour. Carefully drop the squid into the oil and fry for 2–3 minutes until golden and crispy, then remove with a slotted spoon. Drain on paper towels and keep them warm while you cook the rest.

Transfer the squid to 4 serving plates, sprinkle with parsley and serve immediately with lemon wedges and Lemon and herb mayonnaise.

For stir-fried squid, prepare and season the squid as above. Stir-fry in 6 tablespoons olive oil. Remove, drain and keep warm while you cook 1 sliced onion, 1 sliced green bell pepper, 2 crushed garlic cloves, 1 bay leaf, 1½ cups chopped tomatoes, and ⅓ cup pitted black olives. Return the squid to the pan, sprinkle with 4 tablespoons chopped parsley and serve.

creamy smoked fish gratin

Serves **4**
Preparation time **10 minutes**
Cooking time **20 minutes**

4 **plum tomatoes**, chopped
8 oz boneless **smoked trout fillets**, skin removed
13 oz boneless **smoked haddock fillets**, skin removed
3 oz **Gruyère** or **Emmental cheese**, grated
2 tablespoons freshly grated **Parmesan cheese**
2 tablespoons chopped **chives**
¾ cup **heavy cream**
salt and **pepper**
1 lb **new potatoes**, steamed, to serve (optional)

Arrange the tomatoes over the bottom of 4 lightly buttered individual ovenproof dishes or 1 large ovenproof dish. Cut the fish into chunks and place them over the tomatoes. Top with the grated cheeses and chopped chives.

Pour over the cream, place on a baking sheet and cook in a preheated oven, 425°F, for about 20 minutes until the gratin is bubbling and golden and the fish is cooked.

Serve immediately with steamed new potatoes, if desired.

For creamy cod with shrimp, replace the trout and haddock with 14 oz skinless and boneless cod, cut into chunks, and 8 oz peeled and cooked shrimp. Replace the chives with about ½ cup chopped parsley. Finish as above and serve with mashed potatoes with chopped dill added.

vegetarian

spiced pumpkin & spinach soup

Serves **4**
Preparation time **10 minutes**
Cooking time **30–32 minutes**

¼ cup **butter**
2 tablespoons **olive oil**
1 **onion**, roughly chopped
2 **garlic cloves**, peeled
3 lb **pumpkin**, peeled and
   roughly chopped
1 teaspoon **ground coriander**
½ teaspoon **cayenne pepper**
½ teaspoon **ground cinnamon**
¼ teaspoon **ground allspice**
3 cups hot **vegetable stock**
¾ cup **frozen spinach**
salt and **pepper**

To serve
2 tablespoons **pumpkin**
   seeds, lightly toasted
4 teaspoons **pumpkin**
   seed oil

Heat the butter and oil in a large, heatproof casserole and add the onion and garlic. Cook over a medium heat for 5–6 minutes until soft and golden.

Add the pumpkin and continue cooking for an additional 8 minutes, stirring frequently, until beginning to soften and turn golden. Add the spices and cook for 2–3 minutes, making sure that the pumpkin is well coated.

Pour in the hot stock and bring to a boil, then reduce the heat, cover, and allow to bubble gently for about 15 minutes until the pumpkin is soft.

Use a hand-held blender to blend the pumpkin until smooth, then stir in the spinach. Reheat for about 5 minutes until the spinach has melted and the soup is hot. Season to taste.

Spoon the soup into bowls, sprinkle with the lightly toasted pumpkin seeds and a drizzle of pumpkin oil and serve immediately.

For butternut, spinach, & coconut soup, use 1 lb butternut squash, peeled, seeded, and cubed, instead of the pumpkin and cook as above. Stir in ¾ cup coconut milk before serving.

fennel & lemon soup

Serves **4**

Preparation time **20 minutes**, plus chilling

Cooking time **25 minutes**

3 tablespoons **olive oil**

3 fat **scallions**, chopped

8 oz **fennel bulb**, trimmed, cored, and thinly sliced

1 **potato**, diced

finely grated zest and juice of 1 **lemon**

about 7 cups hot **vegetable stock**

pepper

Gremolata

1 small **garlic clove**, finely chopped

finely grated zest of 1 **lemon**

4 tablespoons chopped **parsley**

16 **black olives**, pitted and chopped

Heat the oil in a large saucepan, add the scallions, and cook for 5 minutes or until beginning to soften. Add the fennel, potato, and lemon zest and cook for 5 minutes until the fennel begins to soften. Pour in the stock and bring to a boil. Reduce the heat, cover, and simmer for about 15 minutes or until the ingredients are tender.

Meanwhile, make the gremolata. Mix together the garlic, lemon zest, and parsley, then stir the chopped olives into the mixture. Cover and chill.

Blend the soup in a food processor or blender and pass it through a sieve. The soup should not be too thick, so add more stock if necessary. Return it to the rinsed pan and warm through. Taste and season with pepper and plenty of lemon juice. Pour into warm bowls and sprinkle each serving with gremolata, to be stirred in before eating. Serve with slices of toasted crusty bread, if desired.

For lima bean & fennel soup, heat 3¾ cups vegetable stock with 2 trimmed, cored, and sliced fennel bulbs, 1 sliced onion, 1 sliced carrot, 1 sliced zucchini and 2 crushed garlic cloves. Boil gently for 20 minutes, then add 2 x 13½ oz cans lima beans and a 13½ oz can chopped tomatoes. Heat, stir in 2 tablespoons chopped sage, process to blend, and serve.

fava bean salad

Serves **4**
Preparation time **10 minutes**
Cooking time **20 minutes**

2 **eggplants**, thinly sliced into
   rounds
2 **yellow zucchini**, thinly
   sliced lengthwise
4–6 tablespoons **olive oil**
1⅔ cups **frozen baby fava
   beans**
1 tablespoon chopped **dill**
1 tablespoon chopped **mint**
1 small **fennel bulb**, thinly
   sliced
7 oz **feta cheese**, crumbled
salt and **pepper**
mint leaves, to garnish
1 **lemon**, cut into wedges,
   to serve

Brush the eggplants and zucchini with oil and cook in a griddle pan for 2–3 minutes on each side until soft and golden. You will have to do this in several batches.

Cook the fava beans in boiling water until tender. Drain and toss with 1 tablespoon of the oil, the herbs, and plenty of seasoning.

Allow the fava beans, eggplants, and zucchini to cool before assembling or serve them as a warm salad. Arrange the eggplant and zucchini slices on serving plates, sprinkle with the fava beans and sliced fennel and then the feta. Sprinkle with a few mint leaves and serve with lemon wedges.

For fava bean & celeriac salad, replace the zucchini with 2 thinly sliced red bell peppers and the fennel with 8 oz coarsely grated celeriac.

papaya & lime salad

Serves **4**
Preparation time **15 minutes**
Cooking time **3–5 minutes**

3 firm, ripe **papayas**
2 **limes**
2 teaspoons **light brown sugar**
⅓ cup **blanched almonds**, toasted
lime wedges, to garnish

Cut the papayas in half, scoop out the seeds, and discard. Peel the halves, roughly dice the flesh, and place in a bowl.

Finely grate the zest of both limes, then squeeze one of the limes and reserve the juice. Cut the pith off the second lime and segment the flesh over the bowl of diced papaya to catch the juice. Add the lime segments and grated zest to the papaya.

Pour the lime juice into a small saucepan with the sugar and heat gently until the sugar has dissolved. Remove from the heat and allow to cool.

Pour the cooled lime juice over the fruit and toss thoroughly. Add the toasted almonds and serve with lime wedges.

For papaya & lime yogurt, use 1 papaya and 1 lime. Prepare the papaya as above, omitting the segments and syrup. Chop the almonds. Mix with 1¾ cups thick Greek or whole milk yogurt and serve for breakfast with muesli or as a simple dessert, topped with granola. It is also very good as a topping for waffles.

vegetable & cheese wrap

Serves **4**
Preparation time **10 minutes**
Cooking time **6–8 minutes**

7 oz **soft, mild goat cheese**
8 medium-size **soft tortilla
wraps**
16 **basil leaves**
1 cup **grilled artichokes in
oil**, drained
1 cup **grilled eggplants in oil**,
drained
1 cup **grilled sweet peppers
in oil**, drained
8 **sun-dried tomatoes**
⅓ cup **pine nuts**, lightly
toasted
2 cups **wild arugula**
4 tablespoons **Parmesan
cheese** shavings (optional)

Spread the cheese over the tortillas and arrange
the basil leaves lengthwise in the center of each wrap.
Top with the vegetables and finish with the pine nuts,
arugula, and Parmesan shavings, if used.

Roll up each tortilla by bringing in the sides and then
rolling the wrap so that the sides are closed and the
filling is concealed.

Heat a large, dry, griddle pan or skillet over a medium
heat. Cook the wraps for about 6–8 minutes, turning
frequently. Remove from the heat, cut each one
diagonally, and serve immediately.

For cheese & tomato wraps with peppers, replace
the goat cheese with a cream cheese with herbs and
garlic. Omit the artichokes and eggplants and replace
the sun-dried tomatoes with 13 oz fresh cherry
tomatoes, which you should halve.

stuffed sweet potato melt

Serves **4**
Preparation time **10 minutes**
Cooking time **50 minutes**

4 **sweet potatoes**
12 oz **taleggio cheese**, sliced
½ teaspoon **dried thyme**
sprigs of **parsley**, to garnish

Caramelized onions
5 tablespoons **vegetable oil**
6 large **onions**, sliced
4 tablespoons **white wine**
3 tablespoons **white wine
vinegar**
1 tablespoon **brown sugar**
1 teaspoon **dried thyme**
salt and **pepper**

Prick the sweet potatoes with a sharp knife and put them in a preheated oven, 425°F, for about 45 minutes or until the flesh is soft when tested with a knife.

Meanwhile, make the caramelized onions. Heat the oil in a large skillet over a low heat and add all the remaining ingredients. Cook slowly, stirring occasionally, for about 30 minutes until the onions are nut brown and soft.

Remove the potatoes from the oven and put them on a baking sheet. Carefully slice the potatoes in half and pile over the caramelized onions. Top with the sliced taleggio and a sprinkling of thyme and cook under a preheated hot broiler for 4–5 minutes until bubbling and beginning to brown.

Garnish with sprigs of parsley and serve immediately with a crisp green salad and a dollop of sour cream, if desired.

For polenta with caramelized onions & goat cheese rounds, cut 2 x 1 lb packages of ready-made polenta into 8 slices and cut 2 x 4 oz goat cheeses into 4 slices each. Broil the polenta slices on one side. Turn them over and top each one with some caramelized onions, prepared as above, and 1 slice of goat cheese. Return to the broiler for about 5 minutes, until the cheese is brown on top and soft.

144

spinach & sweet potato cakes

Serves **4**

Preparation time **35 minutes**, plus infusing

Cooking time **about 40 minutes**

1 lb **sweet potatoes**, peeled and cut into chunks

2½ cups **spinach leaves**

4–5 **scallions**, finely sliced

olive oil, for deep-frying

3 tablespoons **sesame seeds**

4 tablespoons **all-purpose flour**

salt and **pepper**

Red chili & coconut dip

¾ cup **coconut cream**

2 **red chilies**, seeded and finely chopped

1 **lemon grass stalk**, thinly sliced

3 **kaffir lime leaves**, shredded

small bunch of **cilantro**, chopped

2 tablespoons **sesame oil**

To garnish

lime wedges

scallions, shredded

Cook the sweet potatoes in lightly salted boiling water for about 20 minutes or until tender. Drain, then return them to the pan and place over a low heat for 1 minute, stirring constantly, so the excess moisture evaporates. Lightly mash the potatoes with a fork.

Meanwhile, put the spinach in a colander and pour over a kettle of boiling water. Refresh the spinach in cold water and squeeze dry. Stir the wilted spinach into the potatoes, then add the scallions. Season and set aside.

Make the dip. Gently warm the coconut cream in a pan with the chilies, lemon grass, and lime leaves for about 10 minutes. Don't let it boil. Set aside to infuse.

Heat the oil in a large pan or deep-fat fryer to 350°F or until a cube of bread browns in 20 seconds. Use your hands to form the potato mixture into 12 cakes. Mix together the sesame seeds and flour and sprinkle over the cakes, then carefully lower them into the oil and fry in batches for about 3 minutes until they are golden and crispy. Drain on paper towels and keep warm while you cook the rest.

Stir the cilantro and sesame oil into the dip and pour it into 4 individual dishes. Serve immediately with the potato cakes, garnished with lime wedges and scallions.

For sage-seasoned spinach & sweet potato cakes with apple sauce, shred 6 large fresh sage leaves and add to the potato cakes. Cook 13 oz cooking apples and beat to a puree with 3–4 tablespoons sugar. Add 2 tablespoons melted butter and the zest of 1 lemon. Serve the hot cakes as an appetizer with the apple sauce.

mushroom & broccoli pie

Serves **4**
Preparation time **8 minutes**
Cooking time **30 minutes**

12 oz **broccoli florets**
3 tablespoons **olive oil**
12 oz **mushrooms**, trimmed
and thickly sliced
5 oz **Gorgonzola cheese**
3 tablespoons **mascarpone**
cheese
4 tablespoons **sour cream**
2 tablespoons chopped
chives
1 large sheet ready-rolled **puff**
pastry (thawed if frozen)
1 **egg**, lightly beaten
salt and **pepper**

Cook the broccoli in lightly salted boiling water for about 2 minutes or until the florets are just beginning to soften.

Meanwhile, heat the oil in a large skillet and cook the mushrooms over a medium heat, stirring occasionally, for about 5 minutes. Stir in the Gorgonzola, mascarpone, and sour cream. Add the drained broccoli florets and the chives, season and tip into 4 individual ovenproof dishes or 1 large rectangular ovenproof dish.

Lay the pastry over the filling, pressing it to the sides of the dish to seal. Brush the top with beaten egg and cut two slits. Cook in a preheated oven, 425°F, for about 25 minutes until the pastry is crisp and golden. Serve immediately.

For puff-crust cauliflower cheese pie, use 14 oz cauliflower florets instead of the broccoli and 1¾ cups grated strong Cheddar cheese instead of the Gorgonzola. Omit the mushrooms.

cumin lentils with yogurt dressing

Serves **4**
Preparation time **10 minutes**
Cooking time **13 minutes**

4 tablespoons **olive oil**
2 **red onions**, thinly sliced
2 **garlic cloves**, chopped
2 teaspoon **cumin seeds**
5 cups cooked **Puy lentils**
3 cups **peppery leaves**, such
as beet or arugula
1 large raw **beet**, peeled and
coarsely grated
1 **Granny Smith apple**,
peeled and coarsely grated
(optional)
lemon juice, to serve
salt and **pepper**

Yogurt dressing
1¼ cups **Greek** or **whole milk
yogurt**
2 tablespoons **lemon juice**
½ teaspoon **ground cumin**
¼ cup chopped **mint leaves**

Heat the oil in a skillet and fry the red onions over a medium heat for about 8 minutes until soft and golden. Add the garlic and cumin seeds and cook for an additional 5 minutes.

Mix the onion mixture into the lentils, season well, and allow to cool.

Make the dressing by mixing together the ingredients in a small bowl.

Serve the cooled lentils on a bed of leaves, with the grated beet and apple (if used), a couple of spoonfuls of minty yogurt, and a generous squeeze of lemon juice.

For cumin chickpeas with apricots, use 2 x 14 oz cans chickpeas instead of the lentils. Chop and add ⅔ cup ready-to-eat dried apricots to replace the beet and apple.

asparagus with tarragon dressing

Serves **4**

Preparation time **20 minutes**

Cooking time **about 5 minutes**

3 tablespoons **olive oil** (optional)

1 lb **asparagus**

1½ lb **arugula** or other **salad leaves**

2 **scallions**, finely sliced

4 **radishes**, thinly sliced

salt and **pepper**

Tarragon & lemon dressing

finely grated zest of 2 **lemons**

4 tablespoons **tarragon vinegar**

2 tablespoons chopped **tarragon**

½ teaspoon **Dijon mustard**

pinch of **superfine sugar**

⅔ cup **olive oil**

To garnish

roughly chopped **herbs**, such as tarragon, parsley, chervil, or dill

thin strips of **lemon zest**

Make the dressing. Combine the lemon zest, vinegar, tarragon, mustard, and sugar in a small bowl and season to taste. Stir to mix, then gradually beat in the oil. Alternatively, place all the ingredients in a screw-top jar and shake well to combine. Set aside.

Heat the oil (if used) in a large skillet. Add the asparagus in a single layer and cook for about 5 minutes, turning occasionally. (The asparagus should be tender when pierced with the tip of a sharp knife and lightly patched with brown.)

Transfer the asparagus to a shallow dish and sprinkle with salt and pepper. Cover with the dressing, toss gently, and allow to stand for 5 minutes.

Arrange the salad leaves in a serving dish, sprinkle with the onions and radishes, and pile the asparagus in the center of the leaves. Garnish with chopped herbs and thin strips of lemon zest. Serve on its own with bread or as an accompaniment to a main dish.

For garlic & mustard dressing as an alternative to tarragon and lemon, place in a screw-top jar 1 finely chopped small garlic clove, 1 finely chopped small shallot, 2 tablespoons wholegrain mustard, a pinch each of salt, pepper, and sugar, ½ cup olive oil, and 2–3 tablespoons shallot or red wine vinegar. Place the lid on the jar and shake until the ingredients are well combined. Serve drizzled over the asparagus.

curried dhal with spinach

Serves **4**
Preparation time **5 minutes**
Cooking time **15 minutes**

2½ cups **red lentils**
½ cup **butter**
1 **onion**, sliced
1 **garlic clove**, crushed
2 tablespoons **cider vinegar**
1 tablespoons **ground coriander**
1 teaspoon **turmeric**
1 teaspoon **ground cumin**
2 tablespoons medium **curry powder**
½ teaspoon **chili powder**
4 cups **spinach**, chopped
1 teaspoon **garam masala**
salt and **pepper**

To serve
8 **chapattis**
mango chutney

Cook the lentils in plenty of unsalted boiling water for about 12 minutes or until they are soft but holding their shape.

Meanwhile, melt the butter in a saucepan and gently cook the onion for about 8 minutes until it is softened but not browned. Add the garlic and cook for 1 minute, then stir in the vinegar and all the spices except the garam masala and fry gently for 2 minutes.

Drain the lentils and stir them into the spice mix with the chopped spinach. Heat until the spinach has wilted and the lentils are hot. Season to taste, stir in the garam masala, and serve immediately with plenty of chapattis and mango chutney.

For potato & spinach curry, dice 1 lb potatoes and cook them for 10 minutes, until just tender and substitute for the lentils. Increase the quantity of spinach to 1 lb. Serve sprinkled with toasted, chopped cashew nuts.

herby chickpea fatoush

Serves **4**

Preparation time **15 minutes**

Cooking time **4 minutes**

3 **pita breads**

1 **garlic clove**, peeled and
halved

1 **green bell pepper**, cored,
seeded, and thinly sliced

10–12 **radishes**, thinly sliced

13 oz can **chickpeas**, rinsed
and drained

¼ cup chopped **parsley**

¼ cup chopped **mint**

2 ripe **tomatoes**, seeded and
sliced

½ **red onion**, finely chopped,
or 4 **scallions**, finely sliced

½ **cucumber**, seeded
and diced

5 tablespoons **olive oil**

3 tablespoons **lemon juice**

1 tablespoon **tahini** (optional)

1 teaspoon **sumac** (optional)

8 romaine **lettuce leaves**, to
serve

Heat a griddle pan and toast the pita breads for
2 minutes on each side until crisp and slightly charred.
Remove from the pan and rub immediately with the
cut garlic. Cut the bread into squares.

Combine the pita cubes with the bell pepper,
radishes, chickpeas, parsley, mint, tomatoes, onion,
and cucumber. Pour over the oil and lemon juice and
stir in the tahini (if used). Mix until the salad is well
coated. Tip into a serving dish and sprinkle with the
sumac (if used).

Put 2 lettuce leaves on each serving plate and let
people help themselves to the fatoush.

For cannellini & French bread salad, replace the pita
bread with French bread cubes, baked in a preheated
oven, 350°F, for about 15 minutes until crisp and
browning. Use cannellini beans instead of chickpeas
and replace the tahini with 2 tablespoons pesto. Omit
the sumac and garlic.

tabbouleh with fruit & nuts

Serves **4**

Preparation time **10 minutes**, plus soaking

¾ cup **bulghur wheat**

¾ cup **unsalted, shelled pistachio nuts**

1 small **red onion**, finely chopped

3 **garlic cloves**, crushed

½ cup chopped **flat leaf parsley**

¼ cup chopped **mint**

finely grated zest and juice of 1 **lemon** or **lime**

1 cup **ready-to-eat prunes**, sliced

4 tablespoons **olive oil**

salt and **pepper**

Put the bulghur wheat in a bowl, cover with plenty of boiling water and allow to soak for 15 minutes.

Meanwhile, put the nuts in a separate bowl and cover with boiling water. Allow to stand for 1 minute, then drain. Rub the nuts between several thicknesses of paper towels to remove most of the skins, then peel away any remaining skins with your fingers.

Mix the nuts with the onion, garlic, parsley, mint, lemon or lime zest and juice, and prunes in a large bowl.

Drain the bulghur wheat thoroughly in a sieve, pressing out as much moisture as possible with the back of a spoon. Add to the other ingredients with the oil and toss together. Season to taste with salt and pepper and chill until ready to serve.

For classic tabbouleh, omit the nuts and prunes and add 6 chopped tomatoes and ⅓ cup black olives, chopped. Use only 2 garlic cloves and be sure to use a lemon not a lime.

haloumi with cucumber salad

Serves **4**
Preparation time **10 minutes**
Cooking time **5–6 minutes**

1 **cucumber**, sliced into long,
   thin ribbons
20 Greek-style pitted **black
   olives**
2 tablespoons chopped
   parsley
2 tablespoons chopped **mint**
1 **green bell pepper**, cored,
   seeded, and diced
8 **radishes**, sliced into thin
   batons
2 **scallions**, thinly sliced
   (optional)
4 tablespoons **olive oil**
2 tablespoons **lemon juice**
8 thick slices of **country-style
   bread**
8 oz **haloumi cheese**, sliced
1 tablespoon finely grated
   lemon zest
pepper

Combine the cucumber, olives, herbs, bell pepper,
radishes, and scallions (if used) with 3 tablespoons of
the oil and the lemon juice. Season with pepper and
set aside.

Heat a skillet or griddle pan to medium-hot and toast
the bread for 1–2 minutes on each side until golden
and slightly charred. Toss the cheese in the remaining
oil and lemon zest and season with pepper, add to
the pan and cook for 3–4 minutes, turning once,
until golden.

Put a cheese slice on top of each piece of toast and
serve with the salad.

For tomato, mint, & avocado salad, roughly chop
4 ripe plum tomatoes, very finely slice ½ red onion,
and roughly dice 1 ripe but firm avocado. Gently
toss all the ingredients in 2 tablespoons olive oil,
with 2 tablespoons chopped fresh mint and the juice
of ½ lemon.

orange & avocado salad

Serves **4**
Preparation time **15 minutes**

4 large juicy **oranges**
2 small ripe **avocados**, peeled
  and pitted
2 teaspoons **cardamom pods**
3 tablespoons **light olive oil**
1 tablespoon **honey**
pinch of **ground allspice**
2 teaspoons **lemon juice**
salt and **pepper**
sprigs of **watercress**,
  to garnish

Cut the skin and the white membrane off the oranges. Working over a bowl to catch the juice, cut between the membranes to remove the segments. Slice the avocados and toss gently with the orange segments. Pile onto serving plates.

Reserve a few whole cardamom pods for garnishing. Crush the remainder using a mortar and pestle to extract the seeds or place them in a small bowl and crush with the end of a rolling pin. Pick out and discard the pods.

Mix the seeds with the oil, honey, allspice, and lemon juice. Season to taste and stir in the reserved orange juice. Garnish the salads with sprigs of watercress and the reserved cardamom pods and serve with the dressing spooned over the top.

For orange & walnut salad, separate the segments from 2 large oranges as above and mix them with 1 crushed garlic clove, ½ cup chopped walnut halves and 4 thinly sliced heads of chicory. Stir in 3 tablespoons walnut oil and ½ teaspoon superfine sugar. Decorate with whole walnuts and serve.

asparagus & snow pea stir-fry

Serves **4**

Preparation time **10 minutes**

Cooking time **7–9 minutes**

2 tablespoons **vegetable oil**

3 oz **fresh ginger root**, peeled
and thinly shredded

2 large **garlic cloves**, thinly
sliced

4 **scallions**, diagonally sliced

8 oz thin **asparagus spears**,
cut into 1¼ inch lengths

5 oz **snow peas**, cut in half
diagonally

2½ cups **bean sprouts**

3 tablespoons **light soy
sauce**

To serve

steamed rice

extra **soy sauce** (optional)

Heat a large wok until it is smoking then add the oil.
Stir-fry the ginger and garlic for 30 seconds, add the
scallions and cook for an additional 30 seconds. Add
the asparagus and cook, stirring frequently, for another
3–4 minutes.

Add the snow peas and cook for 2–3 minutes until
the vegetables are still crunchy but beginning to soften.
Finally, add the bean sprouts and toss in the hot oil for
1–2 minutes before pouring in the soy sauce and
removing from the heat.

Serve immediately with steamed rice and extra soy
sauce, if desired.

For stir-fried vegetable omelets, for each omelet,
beat together 3 eggs with 2 tablespoons water and
seasoning. Cook in a skillet until lightly set (see page
166 for instructions). Top with a quarter of the cooked
vegetables and fold in half. Set aside to keep warm
and make three more.

pea & leek omelet

Serves **4**
Preparation time **5–6 minutes**
Cooking time **19–22 minutes**

8 oz baby **new potatoes**
⅓ cup **butter**
1 tablespoon **olive oil**
1 lb **leeks**, trimmed, cleaned,
   and cut into ½ inch slices
1¼ cups frozen or fresh **peas**
6 **eggs**
⅔ cup **milk**
2 tablespoons chopped
   chives
½ cup **soft garlic and chive
   cheese**
salt and **pepper**

To serve
3 cups **salad leaves**
4 tablespoons ready-made
   salad dressing

Cook the potatoes in boiling water for about
10 minutes or until cooked but still firm.

Meanwhile, melt the butter with the oil in a large
skillet, add the leeks, cover, and cook, stirring frequently,
for 8–10 minutes or until soft. Stir in the peas.

Drain the potatoes, cut them into quarters and add to
the skillet. Continue cooking for 2–3 minutes.

Beat the eggs with the milk and chives, season well,
and pour into the skillet. Move around with a spatula so
that the vegetables are well coated and the egg begins
to cook. Crumble the cheese on top and leave over a
medium heat for 2–3 minutes until the egg becomes
firm.

Place under a preheated hot broiler for 3–4 minutes
until the omelet is completely set and the top is golden
brown. Serve in thick slices with a prepared salad and
ready-made dressing.

For quick herb salad dressing, beat together
6 tablespoons olive oil, 2 tablespoons wine vinegar,
3 tablespoons chopped parsley, ½ grated small onion,
½ teaspoon mustard, ¼ teaspoon superfine sugar, and
a little ground coriander. Season to taste.

wild rice & goat cheese salad

Serves **4**
Preparation time **10 minutes**
Cooking time **about**
  15 minutes

1 ¼ cups mixed **long grain** and
  wild rice
4 oz **fine green beans**
4 tablespoons **olive oil**
3 **red onions**, thinly sliced
⅔ cup **balsamic vinegar**
1 teaspoon chopped **thyme**
4 oz **goat cheese**, sliced
8 **baby plum tomatoes**,
  halved
small bunch of **basil**
salt and **pepper**

Cook the rice in lightly salted boiling water for about 15 minutes until tender or according to the instructions on the package. Add the green beans for the final 2 minutes of cooking. Drain and set aside.

Meanwhile, heat the oil in a large skillet and cook the onions gently for about 12 minutes or until soft and golden. Add the balsamic vinegar and thyme, season with salt and pepper, and allow to bubble gently for 2–3 minutes until the mixture thickens slightly.

Stir the onions into the rice and beans and allow to cool. Once cool, sprinkle with the cheese, tomatoes, and basil leaves and serve.

For pearl barley salad with smoked cheese, replace the rice with the same quantity of pearl barley and cook in boiling water for 25–35 minutes until tender, then drain. Substitute the goat cheese with diced smoked cheese.

potato gratin with chicory

Serves **4**
Preparation time **10 minutes**
Cooking time **43–45 minutes**

3 lb **floury potatoes,** peeled
    and cut into ¼ inch slices
¼ cup **butter**
1 tablespoon **olive oil**
1 **onion,** sliced
3 **garlic cloves,** chopped
1⅔ cups grated **cheddar**
    cheese
1¾ cups **heavy cream** or
    full-fat **sour cream**
12 oz **Reblochon** or **Brie**
    cheese, sliced
salt and **pepper**

To serve
3–4 heads **chicory,** separated
ready-made **French dressing**

Cook the potatoes in lightly salted boiling water for
10 minutes, then drain.

Melt the butter with the oil in a medium saucepan and
cook the onion for about 5 minutes, or until soft and
golden. Add the garlic and cook for an additional
2 minutes.

Add the grated cheese and cream or sour cream. Stir
until the mixture is hot and the cheese has melted.
Season to taste.

Arrange half the potatoes in a lightly buttered, shallow,
ovenproof dish. Place half the cheese slices over the
potatoes and pour over half the cheese sauce. Cover
with the remaining potato slices, the rest of the cheese
sauce, and top with the remaining cheese slices.

Cook in a preheated oven, 425°F, for 30–35 minutes
until bubbling and golden brown. Serve immediately
with the chicory and dressing.

For Italian-style gratin, use 1½ cups grated pecorino
and 13 oz fontina for the hard and soft cheeses.
Sprinkle with a teaspoon of dried Italian herbs and add
1 teaspoon finely chopped rosemary before baking.

beet & squash spaghetti

Serves **4**
Preparation time **8 minutes**
Cooking time **10 minutes**

10 oz dried **spaghetti** or
  fusilli
5 oz **fine green beans**
1 lb **butternut squash**,
  peeled, seeded, and cut into
  ½ inch dice
4 tablespoons **olive oil**
1 lb raw **beets**, cut into
  ½ inch dice
½ cup **walnuts**, crushed
5 oz **goat cheese**, diced
2 tablespoons **lemon juice**
freshly grated **Parmesan**
  cheese, to serve (optional)

Cook the pasta in lightly salted boiling water for
10 minutes or until just cooked. Add the beans and
squash for the final 2 minutes of cooking time.

Meanwhile, heat the oil in a large skillet, add the beets
and cook, stirring occasionally, for 10 minutes until
cooked but still firm.

Toss the drained pasta mixture with the beets, walnuts,
and goat cheese. Squeeze over the lemon juice and
serve immediately with a bowl of Parmesan, if desired.

For baby carrot & squash spaghetti, replace the
beets with the same quantity of baby carrots, cooked
in boiling water for about 5 minutes, until tender.
Roast the butternut squash with 4 garlic cloves
and the oil in a preheated oven, 475°F, for about
40 minutes or until softened. Replace the goat
cheese with havarti or dolcelatte.

italian warm bean linguine

Serves **4**
Preparation time **10 minutes**
Cooking time **12 minutes**

13 oz **dried linguine**
4 tablespoons **olive oil**, plus
  extra to drizzle (optional)
1 **red onion**, finely chopped
2 **celery sticks**, chopped
1 **zucchini**, grated
1 **garlic clove**, chopped
13 oz can **borlotti beans**,
  rinsed and drained
4 tablespoons chopped
  parsley, plus extra to garnish
6 **sun-dried tomatoes**,
  chopped
finely grated zest and juice
  of 1 **lemon**

Cook the pasta in lightly salted boiling water for
10 minutes or according to the instructions on the
package. Drain and set aside and keep warm.

Meanwhile, heat the oil in a skillet over a medium
heat, add the onion and celery and cook for about
8 minutes or until softened and beginning to brown.
Add the zucchini and garlic and stir-fry for a further
1–2 minutes.

Add the beans to the pan and stir in the parsley,
chopped tomatoes, and lemon zest and juice. Cook
for 1 minute, then remove from the heat.

Stir the vegetables into the pasta and serve
immediately, drizzled with extra olive oil and parsley,
if desired.

For crunchy asparagus linguine, whiz 2–3 slices
of white bread in a food processor to make bread
crumbs. Mix well with the finely grated zest of 1 lemon,
1 crushed garlic clove, 2 tablespoons finely grated
Parmesan, and 2 tablespoons pine nuts, season
before toasting in a large skillet with 1 tablespoon
olive oil for 3–4 minutes until golden and crunchy.
Slice 4 oz fine asparagus tips lengthwise and blanch
in boiling water for 1 minute, drain and toss with the
linguine, the juice of 1 lemon, and plenty of black
pepper. Serve sprinkled with the crunchy bread
crumb mixture.

zesty quinoa salad

Serves **4**
Preparation time **15 minutes**
Cooking time **15–20 minutes**

¾ cup **quinoa**, rinsed
1 small **yellow bell pepper**,
    cored, seeded, and diced
1 small **red bell pepper**,
    cored, seeded, and diced
4 **scallions**, sliced
⅓ **cucumber**, seeded and
    diced
½ **fennel bulb**, finely diced
2 tablespoons finely chopped
    curly parsley
2 tablespoons finely chopped
    mint
2 tablespoons finely chopped
    cilantro
2 tablespoons **sunflower
    seeds**
juice and finely grated zest of
    2 limes
8 **cape gooseberries**,
    quartered

Dressing
4 teaspoons **harissa paste**
juice and finely grated zest of
    2 **limes**
8 tablespoons **sunflower oil**
salt and **pepper**

Put the quinoa in a pan of cold water, bring to a boil, and cook for 15–20 minutes or until the quinoa is translucent and just cooked. Drain and rinse thoroughly in cold water.

Meanwhile, make the dressing by mixing together the harissa paste, lime juice and zest, and oil. Season to taste and set aside.

Mix the cooked quinoa with the prepared vegetables and herbs, 1 tablespoon of the sunflower seeds, and the lime juice and zest.

Sprinkle with the cape gooseberries and the remaining sunflower seeds and serve with the dressing.

For baked potatoes with quinoa salad, coat 4 large potatoes, about 14 oz each, with olive oil and salt, prick all over with a fork and bake in a preheated oven, 425°F, for about an hour, until the skins are crisp and a skewer slides in easily. Make the salad as above, omitting the sunflower seeds, limes, and cape gooseberries. Mix ¾ cup sour cream with 2 tablespoons chopped chives and a little nutmeg. Fill the potatoes with the salad and top with the sour cream instead of the dressing.

feta & watermelon salad

Serves **4**
Preparation time **10 minutes**
Cooking time **2 minutes**

1 tablespoon **black sesame
  seeds**
1 lb **watermelon**, peeled,
  seeded, and diced
6 oz **feta cheese**, diced
1¾ lb **arugula**
sprigs of **mint, parsley,** and
  cilantro
6 tablespoons **olive oil**
1 tablespoon **orange flower
  water**
1½ tablespoons **lemon juice**
1 teaspoon **pomegranate
  syrup** (optional)
½ teaspoon **superfine sugar**
salt and **pepper**

Heat a skillet and dry-fry the sesame seeds for
2 minutes until aromatic, then set aside.

Arrange the watermelon and feta on a large plate with
the arugula and herbs.

Beat together the oil, orange flower water, lemon juice,
pomegranate syrup (if used), and sugar. Season to
taste with salt and pepper, then drizzle over the salad.
Sprinkle with the sesame seeds and serve with toasted
pita bread.

For quick feta & tomato salad, mix 1 lb skinned
and chopped tomatoes with 8 oz cubed feta and
⅓ cup pitted black olives. Drizzle over a mixture of
3 tablespoons olive oil, 2 chopped garlic cloves, and
½ teaspoon superfine sugar. Season with plenty of
black pepper and serve.

broiled polenta & cheese bake

Serves **4**
Preparation time **8 minutes**
Cooking time **25–30 minutes**

¾ cup **roasted red sweet peppers in olive oil**
2 lb ready-made, firm **polenta**, cut into ¼ inch slices
5 oz **fontina cheese**, grated
5 oz **pecorino cheese**, grated
1 **garlic clove**, chopped
1½ cups **passata**
1 teaspoon finely grated **lemon zest**
pinch of **superfine sugar**
small bunch of **basil**, shredded, plus extra whole leaves to garnish
salt and **pepper**

Drain and slice the sweet peppers, reserving 3 tablespoons of the oil.

Arrange half the polenta slices in a lightly buttered ovenproof dish and sprinkle with half the sliced peppers and cheeses.

Repeat the layers and cook in a preheated oven, 475°F, for 15 minutes.

Meanwhile, heat the oil from the peppers in a pan and fry the garlic over a medium heat until soft and beginning to turn golden. Stir in the remaining ingredients, season to taste, and bring to a boil, then reduce the heat and allow to bubble gently for 15–20 minutes.

Put the polenta bake under a preheated hot broiler for 5 minutes to brown the top. Garnish with basil leaves and serve immediately with the tomato sauce.

For semolina gnocchi, add 1⅛ cups semolina to 3⅔ cups boiling milk, reduce the heat and simmer for 5 minutes, stirring constantly with a whisk until thick. Add a little butter then pour into a 2 lb loaf pan. Cook in a preheated oven, 350°F, until firm, and slice. Layer and broil as above.

desserts

strawberry gelatin desserts

Serves **6**
Preparation time **10 minutes**,
   plus standing and chilling
Cooking time **5 minutes**

1 cup **strawberries**, hulled
½ cup **superfine sugar**
2 cups **white grape juice**
2 envelopes of **granulated
   gelatin** or 6 **gelatin leaves**
5 tablespoons **crème de
   cassis** (optional)

Roughly chop three-quarters of the strawberries and put them in a food processor or blender with 1¼ cups boiling water and the sugar. Blend until smooth, then pour the mixture into a sieve set over a bowl and stir to allow the liquid to drip through.

Pour ¾ cup of the grape juice into a heatproof bowl, sprinkle with the gelatin and allow to stand for 10 minutes. Place the bowl over a saucepan of simmering water and stir until the gelatin has dissolved. Allow to cool, then stir in the cassis (if used), strawberry liquid, and the remaining grape juice.

Arrange the remaining strawberries in 6 large wine glasses, pour over the liquid and chill until set.

For raspberry champagne gelatin desserts, substitute the strawberries with raspberries and omit the cassis. Dissolve the gelatin in only 6 tablespoons grape juice and, when cool, stir in 1¾ cups sparkling white wine. Finish as above.

chocolate, date, & almond panini

Serves **4**

Preparation time **10 minutes**, plus cooling

Cooking time **26–28 minutes**

3 tablespoons whole **blanched almonds**

2 tablespoons **confectioners' sugar**

3 oz **white chocolate**, finely grated

8 soft **dates**, pitted and chopped

¼ cup **slivered almonds**, lightly toasted

8 slices **brioche**, buttered on both sides

3 tablespoons **heavy cream**, whipped

Put the blanched almonds in a colander and sprinkle with a little cold water. Shake off any excess water and place the almonds on a nonstick baking sheet. Sift the confectioners' sugar over the top and bake in a preheated oven, 350°F, for about 20 minutes until they have crystallized.

Remove the almonds from the oven and set aside to cool, then put them in a freezer bag and tap lightly with a rolling pin until they are crushed but not powdery.

Mix together the grated chocolate, dates, and almonds. Spoon the mixture onto 4 slices of the buttered brioche and top with the remaining slices to make 4 sandwiches.

Heat a griddle over a medium heat and cook the brioche sandwiches for 3–4 minutes. Turn them over and cook the other side for another 3–4 minutes to make a panini.

Cut the panini in half diagonally and serve immediately with whipped cream and sprinkled with the crushed almonds.

For eggy bread, substitute the brioche with sweet French toasts. Dip each French toast in a mixture of 2 eggs lightly beaten with 4 tablespoons milk. Fry in butter, turning, until golden on both sides. Omit the nuts and cream and serve with honey or syrup.

peach & blueberry crunch

Serves **4**
Preparation time **8 minutes**
Cooking time **8–10 minutes**

¼ cup **ground hazelnuts**
¼ cup **ground almonds**
2 tablespoons **superfine sugar**
½ cup **bread crumbs**
13½ oz can **peaches in natural juice**
1 cup **blueberries**
⅔ cup **heavy cream**
seeds from **1 vanilla bean**
1 tablespoon **confectioners' sugar**, sifted

Gently cook the ground nuts in a large skillet with the sugar and bread crumbs, stirring constantly until golden. Remove from the heat and allow to cool.

Put the peaches in a food processor or blender and blend with enough of the peach juice to make a thick, smooth puree.

Fold most of the blueberries gently into the puree and spoon into 4 glasses or individual serving dishes. Set aside a few of the blueberries to decorate.

Whip the cream with the vanilla seeds and confectioners' sugar until thick but not stiff and spoon evenly over the peach puree. When the crunchy topping is cool, sprinkle it over the blueberry mixture, top with the remaining blueberries, and serve.

For apple & blackberry biscuit crunch, peel 1 lb cooking apples and cook with 2–3 tablespoons sugar and 2 tablespoons water. Fold 1 cup blackberries into the apple puree and continue as above, but instead of bread crumbs, use crushed graham crackers. Use the same amount and toast in the same way, but reduce the sugar to 1 tablespoon.

pancake stack with maple syrup

Serves **4**
Preparation time **10 minutes**
Cooking time **6 minutes**

1 **egg**
1 cup **all-purpose flour**
½ cup **milk**
2½ tablespoons **vegetable oil**
1 tablespoon **superfine sugar**
bottled **maple syrup**,
   to drizzle
8 scoops of **vanilla ice cream**

Put the egg, flour, milk, oil, and sugar in a food processor or blender and whiz until smooth and creamy.

Heat a large skillet over a medium heat and put in 4 half-ladlefuls of the batter to make 4 pancakes.

After about 1 minute the tops of the pancakes will start to set and air bubbles will rise to the top and burst. Use a spatula to turn the pancakes over and cook on the other side for 1 minute.

Repeat twice more until you have used all the batter and made 12 small pancakes in all.

Bring the pancakes to the table as a stack, drizzled with maple syrup, and serve 3 pancakes to each person, with scoops of ice cream.

For orange-flavored pancakes, make a batter from 1 cup all-purpose flour, 2 teaspoons each superfine sugar and grated orange zest, 1 teaspoon each cream of tartar and corn syrup, ½ teaspoon each salt and baking soda, 1 egg, ½ cup warm milk, and a few drops of orange essence. Cook the pancakes as above.

quick white chocolate mousse

Serves **4**
Preparation time **5 minutes**,
  plus chilling
Cooking time **10 minutes**

½ cup **superfine sugar**
½ cup **shelled pistachios**
7 oz **white chocolate**,
  chopped
1 ¼ cups **heavy cream**

Dissolve the sugar with 4 tablespoons water in a small pan over a low heat. Increase the heat and boil until it begins to caramelize. Tip in the pistachios and stir, then pour the mixture onto some waxed paper on a baking sheet and allow to set.

Put the chocolate in a heatproof bowl. Heat the cream in a pan until it reaches boiling point, then remove from the heat and pour directly over the chocolate, stirring constantly until it has melted. Refrigerate until cold, then beat with a hand-held electric beater until thick.

Spoon the cold chocolate into serving dishes, decorate with broken shards of the pistachio praline, and serve.

For dark chocolate & orange mousse, substitute the white chocolate with dark chocolate, add ¼ teaspoon orange extract to the melted chocolate and use chopped walnuts instead of pistachios in the praline.

drunken orange slices

Serves **4**
Preparation time **10 minutes**
Cooking time **12 minutes**

4 large sweet **oranges**
3 tablespoons **brown sugar**
3 tablespoons **Cointreau**
2 tablespoons **whiskey**
juice of 1 small **orange**
1 **vanilla bean**, split
1 **cinnamon stick**
4 **cloves**
2–3 blades of **mace** (optional)
ginger ice cream, to serve

Cut off the base and the top of the oranges. Cut down around the curve of the orange to remove all the peel and pith, leaving just the orange flesh. Cut the flesh horizontally into ¼ inch slices and set aside.

Heat 3 tablespoons water gently with the sugar, 2 tablespoons of the Cointreau, the whiskey, orange juice, vanilla bean, cinnamon stick, cloves, and mace (if used) until the sugar has dissolved. Increase the heat and boil rapidly for 5 minutes. Allow to cool slightly, but keep warm.

Heat a griddle pan over a high heat and quickly cook the orange slices for about 1 minute on each side until caramelized. Top with the remaining Cointreau and set alight. Once the flames have died down, arrange the orange slices on serving dishes and drizzle with the orange syrup.

Serve the orange slices immediately with some ginger ice cream.

For nonalcoholic orange slices, slice 6 oranges as above and arrange them in a dish. Cut away the pith from the peel and finely slice the peel. Put it in a saucepan with just enough water to cover. Bring to a boil then immediately refresh in cold water. Place the peel in a clean pan, cover with water, and simmer for 25 minutes. Dissolve ¾ cup superfine sugar in ⅔ cup water, boil for a few minutes and stir in 2 tablespoons lemon juice. Add the drained peel and pour over the sliced oranges. Chill, then serve with ice cream.

chocolate overload

Serves **4**
Preparation time **8 minutes**

8 **chocolate cream sandwich
   cookies**, crushed
2 tablespoons **butter**, melted
2 cups tub softened
   chocolate cookie ice cream
2 tablespoons **runny caramel**
   or **dulce de leche** (optional)
white chocolate shavings,
   to decorate
milk chocolate shavings,
   to decorate

Mix the crushed cookies with the melted butter and press firmly into the base of 4 dessert dishes.

Scoop the ice cream over the top of the cookie base. Drizzle with the caramel or spoon over the dulce de leche (if used) and decorate with white and milk chocolate shavings. Serve immediately.

For chocolate sundaes with raspberries, replace the cookies with 20 mini meringues and omit the butter. Layer the ice cream, meringues, and 1½ cups raspberries in glasses. Drizzle with light cream and top with grated chocolate.

figs with yogurt & honey

Serves **4**
Preparation time **5 minutes**
Cooking time **10 minutes**

8 ripe **figs**
4 tablespoons **plain yogurt**
2 tablespoons **honey**

Slice the figs in half and place on a hot griddle pan, skin-side down. Sear for 10 minutes until the skins begin to blacken, then remove.

Arrange the figs on 4 plates and serve with a spoonful of yogurt and some honey spooned over the top.

For brioche French toasts with figs, yogurt, & honey, brush 4 slices brioche with a mixture of ¼ cup melted butter and 3 tablespoons cream and toast under a broiler. Top with figs, as above.

nutty cinnamon risotto

Serves **4**
Preparation time **5 minutes**
Cooking time **25 minutes**

½ cup **pecan nuts**
½ cup **hazelnuts**
¼ cup **butter**
½ cup **risotto rice**
5 teaspoons **brown sugar**
1 teaspoon **ground cinnamon**
2½ cups hot **milk**

Heat a skillet over a medium heat and dry-fry the nuts until golden. Remove and set aside.

Melt the butter in a medium saucepan, add the rice and cook, stirring, for 1 minute.

Stir 4 teaspoons of the sugar and the cinnamon into the hot milk, then start adding the milk to the rice, adding a little more once each addition has been absorbed. This should take about 20 minutes, when the rice should be soft but still with a little bite.

Spoon the risotto into serving bowls.

Blitz the nuts in a food processor with the remaining teaspoon of sugar, then sprinkle the mix over the top of the risotto. Serve immediately.

For apricot, citrus, & almond risotto, replace the pecan nuts with ½ cup chopped ready-to-eat dried apricots, and the hazelnuts with ⅔ cup toasted almonds and 2 tablespoons chopped Italian mixed candied peel.

blood-orange sorbet

Serves **4–6**
Preparation time **25 minutes**,
    plus chilling and freezing
Cooking time **about
    20 minutes**

1 cup **superfine sugar**
pared peel of 2 **blood
    oranges**
1¼ cups **blood orange juice**
chilled **Campari**, to serve
    (optional)
orange peel, to decorate

Heat the sugar over a low heat in a small saucepan with 1 cup water, stirring occasionally until completely dissolved.

Add the orange peel and increase the heat. Without stirring, boil the syrup for about 12 minutes and then set aside to cool completely.

When it is cold, strain the sugar syrup over the orange juice and stir together. Refrigerate for about 2 hours until really cold.

Pour the chilled orange syrup into an ice cream machine and churn for about 10 minutes. When the sorbet is almost frozen, scrape it into a plastic container and put it in the freezer compartment for an additional hour until completely frozen. Alternatively, pour the chilled orange syrup into a shallow metal container and put it in the freezer for 2 hours. Remove and beat with a hand-held beater whisk or balloon whisk, breaking up all the ice crystals. Return it to the freezer and repeat this process every hour or so until frozen.

Serve scoops of sorbet with a splash of chilled Campari, if desired, and decorate with thin strips of orange peel.

For papaya & lime sorbet, dissolve ½ cup superfine sugar in ⅔ cup water. Boil for 5 minutes, then set aside to cool. Seed, peel, and dice the flesh of 1 ripe papaya. Process the papaya with the cooled sugar syrup. Stir in the grated zest and juice of 2 limes, chill, and proceed as above.

rhubarb & raspberry crumble

Serves **4**
Preparation time **10 minutes**
Cooking time **25 minutes**

1¾ cups **all-purpose flour**
pinch of **salt**
⅔ cup **unsalted butter**
1 cup **brown sugar**
1 lb fresh or frozen **rhubarb**
    (thawed if frozen), sliced
1 cup fresh or frozen
    raspberries
3 tablespoons **orange juice**
raspberry ripple ice cream,
    to serve

Put the flour and salt in a bowl, add the butter and blend with the fingertips until the mixture resembles bread crumbs. Stir in ⅔ cup of the sugar.

Mix together the fruits, the remaining sugar, and orange juice and tip into a buttered dish. Sprinkle with the topping and cook in a preheated oven, 400°F, for about 25 minutes or until golden brown and bubbling.

Remove and serve hot with raspberry ripple ice cream.

For apple & blackberry crumble, substitute the rhubarb and raspberries with 1 lb apples, peeled and chopped, and 3 cups blackberries. You could also use 1 lb plums, pitted and quartered, and 4 peeled and thinly sliced ripe pears.

chocolate & raspberry soufflés

Serves **4**
Preparation time **10 minutes**
Cooking time **13–18 minutes**

4 oz **dark chocolate**
3 **eggs**, separated
½ cup **self-rising flour**, sifted
3 tablespoons **superfine sugar**
1¼ cups **raspberries**, plus extra to serve (optional)
confectioners' sugar, sifted, to decorate

Break the chocolate into squares and put them in a large heatproof bowl over a saucepan of simmering water. Leave until melted, then remove from the heat and allow to cool a little. Beat in the egg yolks and fold in the flour.

Beat the egg whites and superfine sugar in a medium bowl until they form soft peaks. Beat a spoonful of the egg whites into the chocolate mixture to loosen it before gently folding in the rest.

Put the raspberries into 4 lightly greased ramekins, pour over the chocolate mixture and cook in a preheated oven, 375°F, for 12–15 minutes until the soufflés have risen.

Sprinkle the soufflés with confectioners' sugar and serve with extra raspberries, if desired.

For white chocolate & mango soufflés, substitute the dark chocolate with white chocolate and the raspberries with 1 mango, peeled, pitted, diced, and divided among the ramekins.

summer fruit crunch

Serves **4–6**
Preparation time **10 minutes**
Cooking time **20 minutes**

½ cup **rolled oats**
½ teaspoon **ground cinnamon**
½ teaspoon **mixed spice**
pinch of **ground ginger**
1 tablespoon **butter**, melted
1 tablespoon **honey**
2 tablespoons **golden raisins**
2⅔ cups mixed fresh or frozen
    summer fruits
½ cup **confectioners' sugar**,
    plus extra to garnish
2 tablespoons **crème de**
    cassis
½ teaspoon **vanilla extract**
1 tablespoon **slivered**
    almonds, toasted, to garnish

Mix the oats and spices with the melted butter and honey until well combined.

Press onto a baking sheet and cook in a preheated oven, 350°F, for 20 minutes, turning once. Remove and allow to cool before mixing in the golden raisins.

Meanwhile, put the summer fruits in a pan with the confectioners' sugar and 1 tablespoon water. Warm over a medium-low heat, stirring occasionally, until the fruit begins to collapse. Remove from the heat and stir in the crème de cassis and vanilla extract.

Spoon the fruit into dishes and sprinkle with the crunchy topping. Garnish with the toasted almonds and a sprinkling of confectioners' sugar. Serve immediately.

For fall plum crunch, pit and quarter 1 lb plums and use instead of the summer fruits. Cook the plums in ½ cup apple juice until just tender. Substitute the crème de cassis with sloe gin. Spoon into the dishes and finish as above.

baked lemon custards

Serves **4**

Preparation time **10 minutes**,
  plus infusing

Cooking time **about 1 hour**

12 **bay leaves**, bruised

2 tablespoons finely grated
  lemon zest

6 tablespoons **heavy cream**

4 **eggs**, plus 1 **egg yolk**

⅔ cup **superfine sugar**

6 tablespoons **lemon juice**

Put the bay leaves, lemon zest, and cream in a small saucepan and heat gently until it reaches boiling point. Remove immediately from the heat and set aside for 2 hours to infuse.

Beat together the eggs, egg yolk, and sugar until the mixture is pale and creamy, then beat in the lemon juice. Strain the cream mixture through a fine sieve into the egg mixture and stir until combined. Set aside 4 bay leaves for decoration.

Pour the custard into 4 individual ramekins and place on a baking sheet. Cook in a preheated oven, 250°F, for 50 minutes or until the custards are almost set in the middle. Allow to stand until cold, then chill until required. Allow to return to room temperature before serving, decorated with the reserved bay leaves.

For plain baked custard, mix 1 tablespoon superfine sugar with 1 egg, ⅔ cup warm milk, and a pinch of salt. Use the mixture to fill 1 pie shell or 12 small tart shells made from 8 oz shortcrust pastry, pricked and baked blind in a preheated oven, 400°F, for 20–25 minutes. Sprinkle with grated nutmeg and bake in a preheated oven, 400°F, for about 20 minutes.

hot brioche with chocolate sauce

Serves **4**

Preparation time **5 minutes**

Cooking time **12 minutes**

4 oz **dark chocolate**

1 tablespoon **corn syrup**

½ cup **butter**

4 tablespoons **heavy cream**

4 thick slices **brioche**

¾ cup **Demerara sugar**

4 scoops **vanilla** or **praline ice cream**

2 tablespoons **slivered almonds**, lightly toasted

Put the chocolate in a small saucepan with the corn syrup, 2 tablespoons of the butter, and the cream and heat, stirring occasionally, until shiny and melted.

Meanwhile, melt the remaining butter and brush it over the brioche slices. Sprinkle with the sugar.

Heat a large skillet over a low heat and cook the brioche slices in the pan for 3–4 minutes on each side until golden and crispy.

Serve hot, with a scoop of ice cream, the warm chocolate sauce, and a sprinkling of nuts.

For quick ice cream brioche, serve 4 individual brioches cut in half and arranged on 4 dessert plates with a scoop of chocolate ice cream, whipped cream, and a sprinkling of roughly chopped chocolate chips.

212

upside-down grapefruit cakes

Serves **6**
Preparation time **15 minutes**
Cooking time **about**
  40 minutes

1 **grapefruit**, peeled and cut
  into 6 thin slices
6 tablespoons **corn syrup**
¾ cup **unsalted butter**, at
  room temperature
1¼ cups **brown sugar**
2 **eggs**
1½ cups **self-rising flour**
pinch of **salt**
finely grated zest of **1 lime**
2 tablespoons **grapefruit**
  juice
2–3 tablespoons **milk**

Push a slice of grapefruit to the base of each of
6 buttered pudding molds or ramekins and drizzle
with a tablespoon of corn syrup. Set aside.

Cream together the butter and sugar until light and
fluffy. Add the eggs, one at a time, beating well until
incorporated. Gently fold in the flour, salt, and lime zest,
then fold in the grapefruit juice and milk so that the
mixture has a good dropping consistency.

Spoon the mixture into the molds or ramekins and
smooth down.

Put the molds in a large roasting pan half-filled with
boiling water and cook in a preheated oven, 350°F, for
about 40 minutes or until risen and golden.

Remove the cakes from the oven, lift them out of the
hot water and allow to cool for 5 minutes. Loosen the
sides of the cakes by running a knife around the inside
of the molds and then turn them out into serving bowls.
Serve immediately with cream.

For crème anglaise to serve as an accompaniment
for a special occasion, heat 2 cups milk with a split
vanilla bean to boiling point. Remove from the heat.
Beat together 6 egg yolks and ½ cup superfine sugar,
then slowly beat in the hot milk. Return to the heat
and stir continuously until the custard thickens.
Remove the vanilla bean and serve.

muffin trifle with boozy berries

Serves **4**
Preparation time **15 minutes**

3 cups fresh **mixed berries**,
   such as strawberries, red
   currants, and raspberries,
   plus extra to decorate
3 tablespoons **crème de
   cerises** or **cherry brandy**
1 tablespoon **maple syrup**
2 large **blueberry muffins**,
   sliced
⅔ cup **heavy cream**, whipped
   to soft peaks

Put the fruit in a bowl and use the back of a fork to crush it with the cherry liqueur or brandy and maple syrup until well combined.

Arrange the sliced muffins in the bottom of a glass dish. Spoon over the fruit and top with the whipped cream. Decorate with the extra berries and serve.

For Black Forest trifle, slice 1 chocolate jelly roll and arrange in the bottom of a glass dish. Substitute the mixed berries with pitted black cherries. Scrape the seeds of a vanilla bean into the cream before whipping. Finish as above.

chocolate orange brownies

Makes **16**
Preparation time **15–20 minutes**
Cooking time **30–35 minutes**

8 oz **orange-flavored chocolate** or **dark chocolate** with 1 teaspoon **orange essence**
1 cup **unsalted butter**
⅔ cup **superfine sugar**
4 **eggs**
finely grated zest of **1 orange**
1½ cups **all-purpose flour**
pinch of **salt**
1 teaspoon **baking powder**
5 oz **milk chocolate**, roughly chopped
¾ cup **macadamia nuts**, roughly chopped

Put the chocolate and butter in a heavy saucepan over a very low heat and stir until both ingredients are just melted. Remove from the heat, stir in the sugar, and set aside to cool a little.

Pour the chocolate mixture into a large bowl and beat in the eggs, orange zest, and orange essence (if used).

Sift the flour, salt, and baking powder into the bowl and fold in, together with the chocolate chunks and macadamia nuts.

Pour the mixture into a greased and lined cake pan, about 8 x 12 x 2 inches.

Cook in a preheated oven, 350°F, for 25–30 minutes or until set but not too firm. Leave the brownie to cool in the pan, then cut it into squares and serve.

For ginger chocolate brownies, use dark chocolate (not orange-flavored chocolate) and omit the orange zest. Instead, add 1 tablespoon ground ginger to the flour and ⅓ cup chopped crystallized ginger to the chocolate.

apple & raisin pot

Serves **4**
Preparation time **15 minutes**
Cooking time **15–23 minutes**

2 **lapsang souchong tea bags**
1 tablespoon **honey**
3 tablespoons **golden raisins**
3 dessert or cooking **apples**, peeled, cored, and diced
½ teaspoon **mixed spice**
1½ tablespoons **brown sugar**
2 tablespoons **unsalted butter**
⅔ cup **heavy cream**, whipped to soft peaks
superfine sugar, as required
gingersnaps, to serve

Make a strong infusion of tea using the tea bags in 6 tablespoons boiling water. Stir in the honey and golden raisins and set aside to infuse.

Put the apples in a saucepan with the mixed spice, brown sugar, and butter. Remove the teabags from the infusion and pour the liquid over the apples.

Cover and cook over a medium-low heat, stirring frequently, for 15–20 minutes until the apples start to collapse. Crush to a chunky puree.

Stir the heavy cream into the apple puree until well combined, then spoon the mixture into 4 individual ovenproof dishes.

Sprinkle the surface generously with superfine sugar, then place the dishes under a hot broiler until the sugar begins to caramelize. Serve warm or cold with gingersnaps.

For raspberry & rosewater pots with ground almonds, use the back of a fork to lightly crush 2 cups fresh raspberries with 2 tablespoons honey. Stir in 1 tablespoon rosewater and 3 tablespoons ground almonds. Spoon into 4 ramekin dishes and top each one with a generous tablespoon whipped cream before sprinkling with superfine sugar and caramelizing as above.

croissants with chestnut cream

Serves **4**

Preparation time **15 minutes**

Cooking time **2–3 minutes**

⅓ cup **unsalted butter**, melted

4 day-old **croissants**, split in half horizontally

4 teaspoons **brown sugar**

½ cup **sweetened chestnut puree**

½ cup **mascarpone cheese**

2 tablespoons **plain yogurt**

1 tablespoon **honey**, plus extra for drizzling

To serve

chopped **marrons glacés** (optional)

crushed **chocolate-covered coffee beans** (optional)

Brush the melted butter over the cut sides of the croissants, then sprinkle them with the sugar. Set aside.

Beat the chestnut puree with the mascarpone, yogurt, and honey until smooth.

Heat a griddle pan over a low heat and cook the croissants gently, cut-side down, for 2–3 minutes until hot and golden.

Transfer the croissants to serving plates, top with some of the chestnut cream and drizzle with a little extra honey. Sprinkle with a few chopped marrons glacés or crushed chocolate coffee beans, if desired, and serve immediately.

For chocolate cream to serve as an alternative to chestnut cream, substitute the chestnut puree with 4 tablespoons chocolate spread and mix with the mascarpone and yogurt. Omit the honey. After cooking the croissants, spread them with apricot preserves and then with the chocolate cream.

pink grapefruit parfait

Serves **4**

Preparation time **15 minutes**

2 **pink grapefruit**

5 tablespoons **dark brown sugar**, plus extra for sprinkling

1 cup **heavy cream**

¾ cup **Greek or whole milk yogurt**

3 tablespoons **elderflower cordial**

½ teaspoon **ground ginger**

½ teaspoon **ground cinnamon**

brandy snaps, to serve (optional)

Finely grate the peel of 1 grapefruit, making sure you don't get any of the bitter white pith. Cut the skin and the white membrane off both grapefruit and cut between the membranes to remove the segments. Put them in a large dish, sprinkle with 2 tablespoons of the sugar and set aside.

Beat together the cream and yogurt until thick but not stiff.

Fold in the elderflower cordial, spices, grapefruit zest, and remaining sugar until smooth. Pour the mixture into attractive glasses, arranging the grapefruit segments between layers of parfait.

Sprinkle the top with sugar and serve immediately with brandy snaps, if desired.

For orange & black currant parfait, replace the grapefruit with segments from 3 oranges and the elderflower cordial with black currant cordial. Omit the ground ginger and serve sprinkled with chocolate shavings.

sweet chestnut mess

Serves **4**
Preparation time **15 minutes**

1 cup **plain yogurt**
1 tablespoon **confectioners'
  sugar**, sifted
6 tablespoons **sweetened
  chestnut puree**
4 oz **meringues**, crushed
dark chocolate shards cut
  from a bar, to decorate

Beat the yogurt with the confectioners' sugar. Stir in
half the chestnut puree and the crushed meringues.

Spoon the remaining chestnut puree into individual
serving dishes and top with the meringue mess.
Decorate with the dark chocolate shards and serve.

For sweet chestnut crêpes, stir the chestnut puree
into the yogurt. Heat 8 ready-made crêpes according
to the instructions on the package and spread them
with the chestnut puree mix. Roll them up and sprinkle
with cocoa and confectioners' sugar.

lemon drizzle cake

Serves **8**
Preparation time **20 minutes**
Cooking time **22–28 minutes**

5 **eggs**
½ cup **superfine sugar**
pinch of **salt**
1 cup **all-purpose flour**
1 teaspoon **baking powder**
finely grated zest of 1 **lemon**
1 tablespoon **lemon juice**
½ cup **butter**, melted and
  cooled
crème fraîche or **sour cream**,
  to serve

Syrup
2¼ cups **confectioners' sugar**
½ cup **lemon juice**
finely grated zest of 1 **lemon**
seeds scraped from 1 **vanilla
  bean**

Put the eggs, sugar, and salt in a large heatproof
bowl set over a pan of barely simmering water.
Beat the mixture with a hand-held electric beater for
2–3 minutes or until it triples in volume and thickens
to the consistency of lightly whipped cream. Remove
from the heat.

Sift in the flour and baking powder, add the lemon
zest and juice, and drizzle the butter down the sides of
the bowl. Fold in gently, pour into a greased and lined
8½ inch square cake pan and cook in a preheated
oven, 350°F, for 20–25 minutes or until risen, golden,
and coming away from the sides of the pan.

Meanwhile, put all the ingredients for the syrup in a
small pan and heat gently until the sugar has dissolved.
Increase the heat and boil rapidly for 4–5 minutes.
Set aside to cool a little.

Remove the cake from the oven, allow it to rest for
5 minutes, then make holes over the surface with a
skewer. Drizzle over two-thirds of the warm syrup. Let
the cake cool and absorb the syrup.

Remove the cake from the pan and peel away the
lining paper. Place the cake on a dish and serve in
squares or slices with a heaped spoonful of crème
fraîche or sour cream and an extra drizzle of syrup.

For citrus drizzle cake with sorbet, use orange zest
and juice instead of lemon and serve topped with
lemon sorbet.

passion fruit yogurt fool

Serves **4**

Preparation time **8 minutes**

6 **passion fruit**, halved, flesh
and seeds removed

1¼ cups **Greek** or **whole milk
yogurt**

1 tablespoon **honey**

¾ cup **whipping cream**,
whipped to soft peaks

4 pieces of **shortbread**,
to serve

Stir the passion fruit flesh and seeds into the yogurt
with the honey.

Fold the cream into the yogurt. Spoon into tall glasses
and serve with the shortbread.

For mango & lime yogurt fool, omit the passion fruit,
instead pureeing 1 large ripe peeled and pitted mango
with the zest of 1 lime and confectioners' sugar to
taste. Mix into the yogurt and fold in the cream. Omit
the honey.

mint choc chip cheesecake

Serves **4–6**

Preparation time **12 minutes**, plus setting

7 oz **chocolate cookies**

4 oz **mint-flavored dark chocolate**, chopped

¼ cup **butter**, melted

¾ cup **cream cheese**

¾ cup **mascarpone cheese**

¼ cup **superfine sugar**

1 tablespoon **crème de menthe** or **peppermint extract**

2 drops **green food coloring**

⅓ cup **dark chocolate chips**

Put the cookies and chocolate in a food processor or blender and process to make fine crumbs. Mix with the melted butter and press the mixture gently over the base of an 8 inch, round, springform cake pan. Place in the freezer to set while making the cream cheese mixture.

Beat together the cream cheese, mascarpone, sugar, mint liqueur or extract, and food coloring in a large bowl. Stir in three-quarters of the chocolate chips and spoon the mixture over the cookie base, smoothing with the back of a spoon.

Place in the refrigerator to chill for about 1 hour.

Loosen the edge with a knife, then remove the cheesecake from the pan carefully. Sprinkle with the remaining chocolate chips, roughly chopped.

For individual ginger cake cheesecakes, use 4 x 3 inch fluted tartlet pans. Make a base for each cheesecake by pressing a slice of ginger cake inside each pan. Replace the mint liqueur with ginger wine.

index

236

acknowledgments

Executive Editor: Nicky Hill
Editor: Camilla Davis
Executive Art Editor: Penny Stock
Designer: Grade
Photographer: Stephen Conroy
Home Economist: Joanna Farrow
Prop Stylist: Liz Hippisley
Production Manager: Martin Croshaw

Special photography: © Octopus Publishing Group Limited/Stephen Conroy. **Other photography:** © Octopus Publishing Group Ltd/Gareth Sambridge 29, 39, 49, 101, 123, 153, 187, 191, 195, 199, 223; /Gus Filgate 24, 117, 129, 147; /Lis Parsons 33, 57, 63, 73, 107, 113, 120, 137, 141, 163, 179, 203, 211, 215, 219, 225; /Stephen Conroy 21, 57, 99; /William Lingwood 19, 97, 233; /William Reavell 159.